AF662759

AS GOD TO TEMPLE

notionpress.com

AS GOD TO TEMPLE

Praduman Kumar

notionpress.com

Notion Press

5 Muthu Kalathy Street, Triplicane,

Chennai - 600 005

First Published by Notion Press 2014

ISBN: 978-93-84381-15-8

To my wife Uma,
daughter Molika & son Vikalp

PREFACE

During the course of my long service, I got the opportunities to serve at different parts of India and to interact with many persons, having varied experience and views about the functioning of the system in different companies. Writing instinct in me thought to fictionalize all those things in light –hearted manner. Collections of all those writing over period of time eventually ended up in this book.

The book is in two parts. Part I is about confusion and dilemma of a young new incumbent in the Company, eager to learn new things quickly. His meeting with veterans of the Company, their advised and difficulties in understanding of new learning further worsen his woes.

Part II is about expectations and frustration of employees working in a bureaucratic set up and various constraints undermining efficient functioning of the system. In this part, some of the topics are left open ended for readers' inference.

The book is to be read in lighter-vein as this is a work of fiction only.

If buying of this book makes you feel worth of your money and time, only then I will feel genuinely rewarded.

Praduman Kumar

Bureaucrats;

they are dead at 30 and buried at 60

Frank Lloyd Wright

CONTENTS

PART I

JOINING THE CHAOS

"I am new and come here to join, can you guide me to the concerned person?" inquired a young, studious looking person in a single breath, holding a brown envelope in one hand and an old fashioned briefcase in other.

"You should go to Guptaji at first floor," replied a shabbily dressed person, wiping desks of the office lobby, "But you have to wait for sometime as Guptaji has not come yet" continued the shabbily looking person indifferently.

Newcomer had come at sharp 9 am, as written on the appointment letter. But to his bewilderment there was no sign of life in the office even though 15 minutes had passed after 9 am. Strolling around office building and its sprawling surrounding, newcomer thought he never became late in his school and college days.

"Is today holiday?" newcomer suddenly asked

"It is only 9:15 and people will start coming around 9.30 and onwards" replied the same shabbily looking person, named Madan, carelessly busy in cleaning the lobby and table with a whistle, the job he was doing since last 20 years.

"Why people come at 9.30 and afterwards when office time is at 9 am?" inquired puzzled new comer.

Madan saw newcomer curiously from top to toe and replied "Because it is government office and you will not be rewarded if come early or punished if come late" replied Madan casually

New comer was prompted to ask more questions but Medan's casual way of answering restrained him.

Newcomer, named Bhola Ram, B. Ram in short, or simply Ram, as his acquaintances used to call him, was a normal person in all respect.

An ordinary person with ordinary desires like million others. Ordinary physique, semi -urban looks, apparently nothing peculiar or special about him that could make him different from ordinary mass of people of his age.

Simply one more faces in the crowd.

However, ordinary B. Ram had an inordinate quality of asking too many questions. Endowed with innate quality of making other persons uncomfortable by asking practical as well as 'impractical' questions. Questions whose answers couldn't be given but only to be understood.

Trying to find the logics in everything and every time made him many time irritating. His high I.Q (Irritable Quotient) had earned him tag of 'avoid' among his friends in spite of his simplicity and academic excellence.

Mathematical capability had overshadowed his practical ability.

After completion of graduation, he was in search of a good job and after working here and there for small jobs, finally his excellent academic record earned him this coveted government job.

One more lucky passenger who got the ticket to board the 'Grand -Service- Train of Govt.' from the platform of unemployment.

Understandably there was an atmosphere of jubilation in the Ram's home. And who could be happier than Ram's father, retired few years back from government job. After all, who else could know better than him about 'luxury' of being in government job? Work or no work, recession or escalation, flood or drought, any season or reason, your salary is assured on 1st day of the every month.

Eager to 'educate' his son for his new innings, he preached "Dear son Ram, you are starting new and most important innings of your life wherein you have to play for decades. And to play a good innings in government job without being 'hurt' you must always remember that in office boss is everything. Your many 'happiness' depend on him thus never displeased your boss whether you agree or not with him. "As God is to temple so the boss to office; thus you must do all efforts to keep your boss pleased" continued jubilant voice of Ram's father, a 'successful' retired govt. official, proud of his son achievement.

Ram didn't answer but raised his eyes to ask something.

Knowing very well about his son's nature of asking 'irrelevant' and 'impractical' questions, father beckoned him to listen and continued "and other important things in office - don't argue, don't ask question to seniors, particularly to your boss. As you are entering in new and important era of your career you must shun habit of asking useless questions and bottomless arguing".

"There is no harm in inquiring about things that you don't know, that you don't understand" said confident Ram with politeness

"Look, Ram, my son, this world belongs to practical persons, it is only practical person who enjoy life and ruled over others ; impractical or ideal person suffers everywhere and hit hardest in their service life" advised the father with frowning expression as he knew very well that his son lacks "requisite acumen" needed in this practical, hard-core world for "success". Trying to seek logics in everything had made him utterly impractical in understanding the practical things.

"Gupta sahib has come" hurriedly spoken words of Madan brought Ram in present as well as in standing posture from sitting.

"Good morning, sir" Ram repeated the words of Madan

Guptaji nodded his head mechanically and move forward quickly in apparent hurry to enter in his office, hoping that boss would have also not come so far. He didn't mind coming late but abhor to be seen coming late.

Guptaji, I/c of HR, a perfect bald, had shed all his hairs at same place and same section during last 28 years, and had 'managed' his transfer till now. He joined on a lower rank but steadily got all promotions and recently elevated to this post of importance, partly due to his hard work but main credit goes to his remarkable ability to get tuned up with all types of bosses in no time. He was quick in complying spoken words as well as unspoken words of boss. His sense of understanding of unspoken things of boss and giving them top most priority had helped him not only to remain favorite of all types of bosses but also to supersede so many of his colleagues.

"If we pray to God we may or may not get his blessing but if we 'pray' to boss we are bound to be rewarded." Guptaji used to say to his close friends. And he had been rewarded suitably time and again for his 'worship'.

"May I come in, sir?" asked Ram, pushing Guptaji's cabin door gently.

Guptaji, not yet mentally prepared to start office chores, irritably raised his eyes from folded newspaper. Through his broad spectacles he noticed, that a stranger standing between half opened door, holding some brown envelop in his one hand and a shabby looking briefcase type thing in other hand. The young stranger, lean and short, was hesitant but eager to come inside. Guptaji felt that he had seen this stranger somewhere. Half-heartedly he beckoned him to come inside but his mind was preoccupied with the feeling that he had seen this stranger somewhere.

As the stranger was waiting for signal to seat, suddenly Guptaji recollected that he had seen this stranger in the office lobby along with Madan, the big mouth peon, when coming to office. Once again he felt proud of his memory, sharper than his wit, but now fast losing its sheen because of ageing. The ghost of old age has started dawning on him also.

The belonging and appearance of the stranger was suggesting that he might be a marketing representative of some small company. Guptaji made up his mind not to entertain any such person at this point of time, but then thought of some possible gift article this representative might be having in his briefcase

"Yes"? Guptaji's eyes as well as voice asked the question.

"Sir, I am B. Ram, Bhola Ram precisely, I am new appointee and come to join" said Ram in incoherent and nervous voice and put brown envelope in front of Guptaji as a proof of his statement

Guptaji, mind went blank for few moments then suddenly he recollected about the file, received from Head Quarter about the appointment of Bhola Ram in zonal office. However he never imagined that someone would come so early to join. After all file was received only 3 days back while joining time was within 60 days. There was an instant change in Guptaji unwanted gestures towards Ram, and he asked Ram politely to sit down.

Changing colour quickly was hallmark of Guptaji's and it helped him in enduring all types of official storms. Few people could match adaptation power of him.

"Thank you, sir "said Ram as he sat down quietly, looking around in the room.

There were rows of box files placed neatly on the table kept behind Guptaji's chair. On the right side of Guptaji, there were 2 nos. of robust looking steel almirah. Much robust than the only steel almirah at his home, containing some new clothes and little jewellery, which his mother used to takes out either at festivals or wedding of near and dear.

Ram wonders what these robust almirah may have inside.

What name did you say to me?

"B. Ram, Bola Ram precisely, sir" said Ram

"Oh yes" said Guptaji in a soft voice and continued "You are lucky enough to get this job.

After all, now -a- days, it is not easy to get a good govt. job as there are only few seat"

"Thank you, sir "said Ram with polite gesture

There was some jealousy mix pain in Guptaji voice due to the fact that in spite of his best efforts he still could not 'set' his only son in govt. Job, here or in some other company. Though his son got job in few private companies but not able to continue for long due to his high expectation but low competence. Knowing very well about his son 'competence', he was making all round efforts to get him some govt. job but in vain so far. After all, there is enough tolerance for your incompetence and nonsense in Govt. Company. If you are competent in art of pleasing boss, incompetence does not matter much. Even if boss is not pleased you still continue to get the salary as other competent ones. Moreover and it is like traditional Hindu marriage; secured- no clause of divorce.

Suddenly alertness signal rang in Guptaji's shrewd mind, as he completed the sentence "— it is not easy now -a- days to get govt. job as there was few seats".

He had not gone through the personal file of this chap having funny name Bola Ram. And discussing something with someone, without knowing his credentials, was against of his working. Though personal file was received 3 days back from Head Quarter but he had marked it to Radhey, one of his assistant, without going through it for keeping in record. Guptaji could not help feeling irritation on self. He should have at least checked the bio- data of the person coming to join before marking the file to Radhey. Now he had to wait that bugger who used to come at office on his will and convenience.

Ram noticed that Guptaji was impatiently trying to ring someone. During last 5 minutes he has ringed up 3 times but it seems there was no one on other side.

Guptaji's mind was preoccupied for knowing the bio- data, particularly category, of the new appointee sitting in front of him. "Now –a-days you can't judge the person i.e. whether belongs to general or reserved category by his name, like in old days. Things have really become difficult, thought Guptaji, "who knows, he may also have some link with some politician or some big one in Head Quarter otherwise getting govt. job is not so easy"

"I can't take chance. After all I am due for next promotion this year and even a small complaint from any corner ------. There are so many unions, looking for smallest issues to flare them up and there is no one to protect you—"Guptaji's stream of thoughts interrupted by the voice of Radhey, his assistant.

"Good morning, sir, you called me?" asked Radhey in casual manner, chewing something in his mouth, and looked towards Guptaji and then young chap sitting in front of him.

"Bring personal file of Mr. Ram urgently "said Guptaji, though he wished he should ask him why he had come so late but -----.

"I had not received any such file" replied assistant in surprised mixed rebellion voice

"File that was marked to you day before yesterday. Go and check your dak "said Guptaji without losing his calm and composure

Radhey left the room, giving a hard glance to Ram.

One of strength of the Guptaji personality was that he had the extra- ordinary capacity to ignore the contentious issues as well as persons, sometimes at the cost of compromising his ego. He had never tried to 'change' the incorrigible and impudent ones but simply adjusted with them.

"In government office you can't change the people. You have simply learn to go along with them by rewarding or praising good ones, encouraging the normal ones, adjusting the bad ones and simply ignoring the nonsense ones. Govt. Job is a package deal; you can't choose." He used to preach his friends in lighter moments of discussions

Ram, mute spectator of the conversation, wondered what was in store for him in coming days. Though his father gave him enough sermons about culture and working in govt. company but practical is never as smooth as theory and there is always big chasm between them.

True taste of pudding is in eating not in seeing.

After 5 minutes Ram's file was on Guptaji's table. He quickly browsed it and relieved to know that this shabbily looking gentle man, sitting in front of him, hailed from a small town, had excellent academic record and belongs to general category.

"Absolutely harmless guy" Guptaji murmured to self and decided to take his joining in second half, after lunch. Right now he had to go to his boss's room, a 'not to miss' ritual before starting his routine jobs of the day.

And he was in no mood to break his old principle for a new comer.

“Mr. Ram there is a canteen adjacent to this office. Tea and snacks are available there” said Guptaji in relaxed voice.

“I don’t take tea, sir” said Ram politely, eager to learn his job as early as possible

“Ok, have a look around the Bldg. and premise to familiarize—

“Sir, I have already taken a round of the premise in the morning; it is really good “said Ram proudly with the same enthusiasm as he had in college days while finishing work ahead of others to maintain good impression over his teachers.

Guptaji gave a serious glance to Ram through thick glass of his broad spectacle and spoke after a long pause as he was finding himself of loss of proper words

“Look Mr. Ram, you are new here and come to join service. Joining of service requires certain time consuming formalities. There is no point in sitting here. So you can come after lunch” said Guptaji in final words and made postures to leave his chair to stop any further communication at the moment. After all he was getting late. There is no point saying “good morning” to the boss after one hours of coming. Everything had its time and it was the time to meet the boss not to take joining of a new comer.

Ram looked around and left the comfort of the room half-heartedly.

Later, in the comfort of his room, Ram wrote in his diary, a well-preserved habit since his college day to pen the feeling of his disturbed mind.

"It seems that I have come to other end of the world. What a different world here is. It took full day to sign few papers of my joining. People here talk too much and take too much tea. Persons enter in the rooms with files and come out after hours. Guptaji seems to be good person but he lacks the warmth a new person expects. I have been told that my posting or job assignment will be decided after coming of big boss from leave that is after 10 days. Meanwhile to understand the office working and to familiarize, I have been asked to meet all seniors and important section-in -charges one by one. This is good to understand the work but to familiarize----. Anyway, I have to live in this world and it is good to understand things and people as quickly as possible. Though I should rejoice my luck for getting the job in this Govt. Company of repute but somehow feeling of uneasiness is brewing within me.

-Like a new costly shirt with uncomfortable fitting or a new shoes with loose or tight fitting. I don't know what the right comparison is but I have not enjoyed being here today. Perhaps tomorrow will be better."

OFFICE - DECORUM

"As there are formulae in mathematics and laws in physics similarly there are certain rules in office to maintain the office decorum" said white haired Pandeyji to Ram.

Ram nodded but said nothing.

Pandeyji- intelligent, hardworking, soft- spoken and a hard-core opportunist thus endowed with all the requisite qualities needed to be successful in the world. Apart from requisite qualities, he also harbors excessive desire to remain in limelight and to be noticed.

Be it birthday party or funeral, wedding or divorce, Pandeyji had to be there, that too in first row, doing all sorts of activities to remain in focus. Organizing big show, albeit on govt. expense, was another expertise of him.

Pandeyji understood very early in his career that 'requisite qualities' alone are not sufficient to be 'successful' in govt. service thus he decided to follow the formula of '*Be close and confident to the powerful* or at least create such impression'.

A formula that had made him a big manipulator. Everyone around him had the impression that he had big contacts in Head Quarter and also some political backing. Fact was that Pandeyji had none except a shrewd mind beneath white hair.

So, a black haired was sitting in front of white haired.

Naive in front of master manipulator

Lamb in front of wolf

Ram was looking around office of Pandeyji. It was spacious and aesthetically arranged office. Even chair of Pandeyji was bigger than the chair of Guptaji and also there were two telephones on his table. In short, Pandeyji's office was filled with the fragrance of power.

Pandeyji ordered two cups of tea and looked towards Ram. "What was I saying"?

"Sir, you were telling about some rules" said Ram promptly

"Oh, yes. "As you are new here thus you must learn some basic rules to maintain office decorum and cordial relations with everyone" said Pandeyji with an air of authority and continued after brief pause "You know, Mr. Ram, transition from academic to service life is a difficult one due to difference in rules of academic and service life. In academic, output largely depend upon your input i.e. more hard work you do chances of getting more marks brighten or in other words outcome of good or bad result mainly depends on individual's efforts. However, in service life, things are not so straightforward. Here you have to work in a group comprising of boss, senior officers, peers, and subordinates. Even if someone does hard work, may not get 'due output' if he or she doesn't take care of group, particularly, of boss."

Ram was listening Pandeyji's preaching attentively but it was "*Transition from academic to service life*" sentence that caught his maximum attention. Probably due to the fact that Ram was finding it increasingly difficult to overcome this transition.

"I recommend you to read one good book titled "How to manage your boss" said Pandeyji as he lighted cigarette with his gold plated lighter "this book will help in widening your understanding about 'tacit rules' needed to maintain office decorum as well as to grow." continued Pandeyji looking towards broken smoke rings. Blowing smoke rings was Pandeyji's favorite way to relax.

"Sir, I know about rules but never heard of tacit rules"

Pandeyji looked at his wristwatch and then at desk calendar - nothing important to do for another one hour, as one meeting was reschedule.

"Mr Ram, dictionary meaning of Tacit is unspoken; understood without being put into words. Thus tacit rules are the rules not written anywhere but you have to understand and follow them," said Pandeyi in relaxed voice.

"But, sir, if rules are not written anywhere, how it can be understood and practiced properly." said perturbed Ram

"Mr. Ram, you need not to be perturbed. You are new here and will understand everything with time"

"Including tacit rules?" asked Ram

"Very right" said Pandeyji patiently and continued, "For time being, you should remember the following rules of official decorum"

Rule 1

"Never say "NO" to boss.

"Remember, Mr. Ram, any person vested with some power, hate this little word 'NO' advised Pandeyji and continued "If you feel some job can't be done or you don't want to do it then this fact has to be told to boss gradually instead of saying 'NO' at first instance. Whether you agree or not with boss but never say 'Point blank NO' to him. Saying direct NO to boss is like challenging or hurting his ego that too by a junior one, (who is supposed to behave like a white collar slave). As a moneylender never forget the person who owe his money, similarly person in power never forget and forgive the offender of his honour. Remember, boss can digest or adjust someone incompetence but certainly not his / her impudence or disobedience, no matter how competent is he or she".

"But Sir, saying fact or NO to no is not impudence or contempt" said Ram

Pandeyji lit another cigarette. Smell of smoke touched Ram nostril. He never felt comfortable with smoke of cigarettes

"Mr Ram, in boss and subordinate relationship boss is awardees and subordinates remain awarded. Thus, being awardees, boss's ego remains higher than his subordinates and he feels legitimate or legal right over his subordinates. And when ego of someone, inflated with power and right, challenged by some subordinate by saying 'NO' then facts, right, wrong or logics are pushed to back seat by ego."

"Thus never utter 'NO' to boss. If you feel something is not feasible or boss should not ask you to do it even then don't say 'NO' but give the diplomatic answer like "I will see it, sir" or "I will check and let you know, sir" or "it is difficult but anyway I will do my level best, etc"

Pandeyji continued to overwhelm Ram.

(Implicit: *NO is a prohibited word in the un-official dictionary of subordinates)*

Rule 2

"Don't delay personal work of boss. Your efficiency and devotion is at stake. If you are not efficient in boss's personal work how you can be expected to be efficient in official work."

(Implicit: *Boss's personal work has the hidden tag of 'most urgent' thus must supersede all other official priorities*)

Rule 3

"If some important time bound information / report has to be conveyed to boss but you are not able to locate the boss and came to know that boss had gone outside for personal work like market or similar sort of work then don't let boss know that you knew this".

"What should be told to boss after locating him as information was time bound and delay might be considered because of me?"Inquired Ram with childlike innocence on his face.

Pandeyji smiled and said "you have to tell 'Sir I came to your room twice but you were busy somewhere else."

"Mr. Ram, *many times it is beneficial to be ignorant or pretend to be ignorant*. Boss is also a human being and like other normal human being, he may have weakness but no boss want to be exposed to his subordinates. Thus, a veil of pretence of ignorance is to be maintained even though you know all the things about boss. Many good and devoted subordinates suffered due to their over- enthusiasm about knowing everything about boss and their failure to digest it"

(Implicit: Boss likes smart subordinates but no so smart who keep his track)

The authority and fluency of Pandeyji was as good as of some seasoned Professor who got the opportunity of lecturing on his favorite subject after a longtime. Pandeyji would have been much success had he chosen the academic career, thought Ram, who was impressed by the manner of speech rather than content of it. In fact, he was not able to concentrate on the content of speech of Pandeyji.

Pandeyji paused for a while to drink water from the glass kept on side table.

"Sir, may I get one copy of rules so that I can memories them well" said Ram

"A copy, what copy, are you mad" shouted Pandeyji with his eyes wide open in bewilderment.

Ram was more bewildered with the abrupt change in Pandeyji tone and voice ; he was unable to understand what had gone wrong; he used to asked copy of notes in their college day and their teachers never shown their displeasure. In fact the reason of asking copy of rules that he had not been able to concentrate and comprehend what Pandeyji told him. Seeing the strong reaction of Pandeyji he felt it appropriate to apologize, however, he was not feeling comfortable as it was not in his nature to say sorry without feeling it.

"Sorry, sir, I mean ....."

"Look Mr" interrupting Ram rudely and continued "you are not in college but in a government company where things has to be understood even without telling. It is better for you to come out from your theoretical college life and adapt practical life as early as possible. Moreover you are not a kid to whom everything needs to be told; you have to understand the things".

"Yes sir" Ram uttered meekly

Pandeyji was little bit surprised how this boy, who didn't understand simple practical things, had been recruited by Head Office. It looks to him that this chap had some approach of someone at H.Q. In that case, he had to be cautious to avoid trouble. In power game, little carelessness and casualness might cost much. Still memories of Bhatt's case were afresh in his mind. A minor scuffle leads to big crisis when written complaint was made against Mr. Bhatt about harassment of one employee of reserved category, having political links. The matter eventually led to transfer of Bhatt from green pasture to a dry place after a lot of humiliation.

Pandeyji was little bit annoyed with self. Dealing with a new person without knowing his bio data was against his rules. Realizing this, hardened face of Pandeyji become soft

"Look Mr. Ram I did not mean to discourage you; you look bright and intelligent and have good career ahead here. In fact what I mean to say is that you have to learn a lot about office procedure and working culture of the Company" said Pandeyji with best possible politeness in voice as well as softness on face.

Ram was stunned with sudden change in Pandeyji attitude and tone. Perhaps he took his sorry seriously. Ram was trying to find some appropriate words to say without upsetting him again.

"You may come some other time as I have to go in a important meeting and if you required any help you can contact me anytime" said Pandeyji to get rid of him at the earliest as he was desperate to get bio-data of this new –comer before dealing with him any more.

Ram, who was still grappling to find the appropriate words, felt relieved. "Thank you, sir" said Ram as he left the room.

As Ram left the office, Pandeyji immediately rang up to Guptaji, In-charge of the HR department, where personal records of all employees were kept.

"Guptaji,Pandey speaking" said Pandeyji in his polite but authoritative voice. Although both were of same batch but with time Pandeyji had reached in nucleus of power game while Guptaji was still revolving around outer orbit.

"Yes Pandeyji, how are you" said Guptaji in a jealous voice

"Guptaji, I want the bio data of this newly joined chap named B. Ram urgently" said Pandeyji who try to remain courteous with people especially of his batch mate.

"You will get it within five minute. By the way something special" asked Guptaji.

"Nothing particular Guptaji. Just routine. I am waiting for your ring"

How difficult it is to retain what you have got, thought Pandeyji. People like Gupta and others always remain in search to pull him down. Their coating of politeness and softness beneath insidious and harmful intention was not hidden from Pandeyji eyes. Every one of them wanted to take benefit of his position, but never refrained from insidious activity to malign him, to pull the carpet beneath his feet.

Ringing of phone broke his thought process

"This chap is from a small town, having excellent academic record.."Guptaji said without any pause

"Any political reference"

"No" replied Guptaji

"And other thing" asked Pandeyji with gleam in his eyes

"Other things?" asked Guptaji

"I mean category general or reserve" said Pandeyji with little irritation

"Oh, yes he is from general category" said Guptaji who was trying to smell the rat.

"O.K. thank, you Guptaji"

General category, no political reference, good academic record.

Pandeyji was feeling relieved.

That day Ram wrote following in the Diary:

While studying, at entrance gate of college, it was written in bold letter "**Entry for knowledge, departure to serve nation**", but here it appears, allegiance towards boss is bigger issue than serving the nation. My father saying that "As God to temple so the boss is to the office" seems to be true. No doubt Pandeyji eloquence was superb but on asking written copy of the rules, his behavior stunned and bothered me. There are many things here I am not able to comprehend. It looks a nursery student is forced to seat in higher class.

Frankly, feeling of discomfort start brewing over me as I am not enjoying my learning, perhaps my 'transition from academic to service life' will take more time. I can only hope and pray for better time ahead.

Trying to adjust in new atmosphere and learning, Ram started reading newly bought management book to sooth his nerve before sleeping. He noted following paragraph in his diary.

Two relationships are very important for a working person's happiness and growth. The first is the relationship with one's spouse. This is important for happiness. The other important relationship is the one with the boss. This is important for growth of individual. It is wrongly assumed by many that a manager's capability, performance and potential will take him to higher level of management. These factors alone will not be of much help unless relationship with the boss is very good. It is seen that poor boss-subordinate relationship has marred many a career. If this relationship is not managed well, the effectiveness of boss and subordinate suffers. But career wise, the subordinate suffers the most. Therefore, one of the most important functions of a manager in the corporate world is to manage the boss.

ORIENTATION

"Good morning, sir" said Ram, as he entered in the office of Mishra Ji, "I am new appointee here and suppose to report you today for familiarization", continued Ram with copy of order in his hand as a proof of his statement.

Mishra ji, busy in some important file, saw him from pair of his thick glass and after glancing at his wristwatch beckoned him to sit down.

"Sir, my name is B. Ram, Bhola Ram" said Ram quickly as he sat down on one of three chairs in front of Mishraji

Mishraji nodded but said nothing and continued to browse the file, apparently some important one

And, In between

Experienced and naïve one

Age difference of 30 years

Laid a table, bigger than what Ram had in his home.

Three plastics trays, marked with incoming, outgoing and top priority were kept on table. Incoming tray was almost filled with files while outgoing had few one but top priority tray was empty. Some files were very thick and their covers had faded badly and torn up partially. Ram was wondering what these files would be having inside and contemplating to ask about these files but restrained himself as Mishraji was absorbed in reading the file.

"Perhaps, I have come at the wrong time, as Mishraji is too busy or may be in bad mood." thought Ram

However neither Ram came at the wrong time nor was Mishraji in bad mood.

Mishraji, like a seasoned politician, knew very well who should be given importance or not.

Mishraji joined on junior post but over period of time he had been elevated to the level of repute. Mishraji, intelligent and hard working, but much of his intelligence and hard work consumed in analyzing and criticizing rather than doing the things.

A thinker rather than performer.

"This is your first Nokri I mean service" Mishraji spoke at last in his Hindi mix English, without shifting his eyes from file

Mishraji never hesitated to speak in English mixed with Hindi words, which he occasionally supplements by saying 'I mean.'

"Yes, yes sir," replied Ram, almost caught unaware by sudden silence breaking question.

Ram was wondering what would be written in such a thick file. He started feeling apprehensive and scared of his new inning.

"Where is your house, I mean home town" come the next question from Mishraji after a long pause

"Originally I was born in a village but later on shifted to town to pursue my college education as my father -----

"What is your full name" interrupted Mishraji

"B. Ram, Bhola Ram"

"What is your sir name, I mean caste?"

"Sir, all these things do not make any difference to me" said Ram in very polite but confident voice

First time Mishraji observed Ram seriously from his thick glass. Though there was not anything worth eye pleasing about his physical appearance but there was something different, something peculiar the way he spoke.

"Look Mr new, I mean Mr. Ram, you are entering in new phase of your life and in this phase, everything makes difference. Things which you have learnt in your school or college will be of no or little use here" continued Mishraji with his deep voice "Whatever you learnt from your books or college was good enough to pass the examination and getting a job but here, in job, you have to deal not with books but with human beings-the most treacherous creature on earth. And getting along with the people is not as easy as reading few books and passing the examination"

Sign of discomfort had begun to brew on Ram face. He got this job due to sincerity and hard work in his academic phase and aspires to do the same in his new phase of life also. But the tone of Mishraji's words started draining courage out of him and a sense of fear dawned over him.

An invisible crack in the boat.

A chink in his armour.

"You need not to worry" said Mishraji sensing his discomfort "I am not saying you are at wrong place. In fact you are lucky enough to get this job but what I want to tell you that you have to learn a lot of new things and master new skills to get success in your service life also"

Though not having any formal higher educational qualification, Mishraji's I.Q. and understanding of human behavior was far ahead of many educated ones and almost everyone in the office utter his name with respect and savor his philosophical view of life.

"Sir, I will be highly obliged if you let me know what new things I have to learn to get success here" asked Ram with childlike innocence and curiosity in his tone.

There was something peculiar with this new comer. "You cannot ignore his simplicity" thought Mishraji.

Simplicity synonym of stupidity in today world, yet still there are takers of it, though few one.

Thinking whether he should help this new comer or not. His experience with the persons whom he helped more or less was frustrating. Persons who joined many years after him had reached much above of him because of their better qualification rather than better work. What a pity! A 'qualified' donkey was authorized to rule over horses in government jobs. There was no reward of good work and experience but of good qualification thought Mishraji acidly

"What is to be learn to be successful here" asked Ram earnestly.

Mishraji, barely few months away from his retirement, remained silent with forlorn look on his face. 32 years, 32 long years seemed as if few months when he looked back. Naïve, simpleton, and enthusiastic when he joined, used and dumped by almost everyone. Slowly, with bitterness in his heart, Mishraji changed the gear from work to office politics and understood the games people play. And now anyone in office thinks twice before touching Mishraji.

'This simple, untainted boy has to learn the rules of the game to "survive" and has to learn to identify wolf around him in the skin of sheep." *After all lessons of life are tougher than lesson of textbooks,"* thought Mishraji.

"Mr. Ram, office is the place where you have to work with persons of different age groups, having varied qualifications, background, experience and vested interests. Some people come to the office to do the job, as a part of their duty. Some comes to gossip around, to please the boss. Some comes to the office simply for attendances and pass the time. Boss, peers and subordinates are three pillars supporting structure of any office and you have to deal with all of them on day to day basis" said Mishraji and paused to light the cigarette and then continued.

"Dealing effectively with people in office, first you have to learn to understand the orientation of the person you are dealing with."

"Orientation"? said Ram with astonishment on his face

"Yes, people have different orientation at work place. And if you are able to understand their orientation you can deal them in much better way at work place" continued Mishraji in his philosophical style

"How will I identify the orientation of people, sir?" asked puzzled Ram

"Simply observe the people, keep your mouth shut and eyes and ear wide open.

Boss Oriented

"Boss oriented subordinate are very powerful even though they don't have their own strength" said Mishra ji. "They thrive on their boss strength and have only one point agenda- appeasement to the boss. Their allegiance remains for boss not for the company - the bread & butter giver." continued Mishra ji

"Boss oriented persons provides all in and out information of the office to the boss, like secret service agent. They make themselves indispensable to their boss due to their ability of fuelling or satisfying the ego of their boss and capability of showing utmost sincerity in attending personal work of the boss."

'Question of right - wrong, question of conscious does not bother them. What matter for them are the Boss's words'.

Mishraji pause for one minute and said "Here one word of caution for you

Mr. New I mean Mr. Ram and that is - such boss oriented persons should be handle very carefully because they have the ability to influence the decision of the boss in favor or against of you thus You should give them due importance even if you don't like them".

"Boss-oriented persons are like priest of the temple of power. And one must not displease priest if wants to enter in the temple." continued Mishraji in his rare philosophical mood.

Subordinate Oriented

"This rare species believe in developing, grooming and protecting their subordinates. This type of people is usually very popular and has all the good qualities of the excellent boss. Remember Mr. Ram, the subordinated oriented bosses are very possessive about their subordinates thus can go to any extend to protect them. Due to their parental attitude such persons expect full loyalty and obedience from their subordinates" continued Mishra ji "it will be your good luck if you ever get a chance to work under such subordinate oriented personality"

"Unfortunately, subordinate oriented persons are not liked much by their bosses due to their subordinate oriented rather than boss oriented attitude resulting fast extinction of this species"

The vivid analysis of orientation of people at work places overwhelmed Ram and started arousing his interest in the discourse. He never thought that this simple looking person has such in-depth understanding of human attitude at work place.

Work Oriented

"People of this species are the backbone of any company. Wherever posted, they keep on working in one-way or other.. They are the real strength of the company and keep on working just like working ants. These types of people are usually harmless and trust worthy and keep themselves away from office politics. They are real bread and butter earner of the company (and for its parasite also)" "With period of time they become workaholic but never get what they deserve due to inherent lacking in manipulations of the things." said Mishraji in his heart felt voice and continued "Feel yourself lucky if you ever get the chance to work with such people" added Mishraji with gleam in his eyes

Conscience Oriented

Mishraji paused for few minutes, cleaned his spectacles with a crumbled hanky, lit a cigarette and watch the roof of the room for few more minutes before resuming, "Mr Ram, now I will tell you something about a very rare species of office - that is conscience oriented species".

"This harmless but rare species gives more importance to their conscience and honesty than to the work. They cling to honesty and conscience so hard that they forget practical aspect of things and thus suffer very hard mentally as well as practically. They usually take very adamant stance to keep the virginity of their over sensitive conscience intact.

People belong to this species always remain in dilemma of do or don't and many times become real headache for the boss and others who believe in the philosophy of live and let live"

"Though hard working and upright yet hardly get what they deserve due to their grossly impractical and adamant attitude" continued Mishraji with the confidence and conviction of head master of a primary school giving lecture to new entrants.

"The biggest problem with members of this species is the wrong notion about themselves. They feel that they are only honest persons around and people are out to rob their honesty. For them honesty is like virginity and major part of their energy is consumed in protection of 'virginity' rather than doing job or delivering result"

"Mr. Ram avoid working under such bosses because their cynic honesty make them unpopular among higher up which may also dent your reputation in spite of all hard work."

"Sir, it means honesty is not the best policy as I have been taught" asked Ram his first question

"Honesty is still best policy but impractical honesty or rather cynical honesty is certainly not advisable in practical world" advised Mishraji

"True, one should not kill conscience or sell ones honesty but meantime practical aspect of things also has to be seen. Being honest does not mean you become stumbling block to work. Rather I feel that a hard working and output oriented dishonest is much better than a nothing doing cynical honest, doubting and criticizing everybody" continued Mishraji.

Things were getting complicated for Ram. He was not sure whether he should agree with what Mishraji has told or not. He firmly believes in honesty and simply hates the dishonest people. He wants to say something but not getting the proper words to express his view.

Dilemma of Ram was not hidden with experienced Misharji.

"Mr. Ram if you wants to keep your conscience alive and also wants to get your due in this world than remember my final words on this topic. Honesty with the practical aspect of things is good and acceptable but there is no takers of beat of honesty beaten from the impractical drum, no matter how loud it is. People in this world are dishonest as well honest and you have to accept both without any grudge" said Mishraji final words on this issue.

Rules of The Book Oriented

"People of this orientation strongly believe in rule of books rather than work. These "paper collector and signature fancy" always try to take maximum signatures of the people on any damn piece of paper. Their worries are not the work but rules. They can reject a doctor of excellent repute if his stethoscope's specifications does not match with rules of the book. These "helmet wearer in the car" are real pain in the ass of their boss. They enjoy narrating the clauses of the rules of the books to every available person on all possible occasions."

"Mr. Ram, if you ever need a circular / office order/ rules you can approach them" said Mishraji and pause for few minutes for glass of water

Nothing Oriented

"Apart from above major orientation of people towards boss, work, rules, subordinate and conscience at work place there are still good numbers of the people who have inclination or orientation towards none. These 'floating stocks' prefer to remain neutral and adjust themselves as per the situation. They are meant to carry out the work, have very limited aspiration and do the things as they have been told. Easy to mold, easy to control these nothing oriented are the soldiers of any organization. These 9 to 5 duty types never come out from their 'Peon type' mentality irrespective of their post" said Mishraji in monotonous voice as he seems not much interest in this category.

Later in his room, Ram recorded following in his diary, an old habit to note the things in his diary whenever he feel to talk to himself.

I was very happy when I passed my final exam, I was even more happy when I got the offer for job. After all it is not easy to get he job when you have so much unemployment around. But today it seems to me that life has more challenge ahead. I am not able to comprehend fully what Mishraji told me. But one thing is certain this old man, Mishraji, is quite through in his understanding. Sincerity in his speech was much more impressive rather than its words or comments. I have to find out which orientation I belong to or even Mishraji himself. Perhaps a palmist does not know what is written on his own palm.

LEARN TO OBLIGE

"You must learn to oblige important and useful persons to grow," advised Aroraji to Ram

Aroraji, exceedingly courteous, polite and helping but only to his seniors and bosses and 'would be useful persons'.

He never forgot to convey his greetings to important and useful persons on their birthdays or any other occasions. He had meticulously recorded 'useful data' of useful and important persons in his diary.

Name of useful persons due to retired shortly are circled with red pen.

No point in making investment in felling or dead wood. Aroraji knew very well who should be given importance and how long.

With passing of time, Aroraji had mastered the skill of sycophancy and art of obliging the important persons. And till now, he was very successful, got all the promotions in time including others 'fringe benefits'.

Ram, sitting in front of Aroraji, was pondering over what he had been told –'learn to oblige' important and useful persons to grow.

A nursery student in front of head master to familiarize himself about the system and persons.

"If you want to grow you have to learn to oblige important persons around you particularly your seniors and bosses" said Aroraji, in deep and seasoned voice, stressing on each word as he was revealing a big secret.

"Oblige to grow"?

"Yes, my dear" replied Aroraji with gleam in his eyes

"But sir, I think it is hard work and sincerity that is needed to grow" said Ram

Aroraji was dumbfounded for a while with such unexpected response of newcomer. He had overheard that this new chap did not "understand" the simple things but ----

Aroraji thought for a while, removed his spectacles, cleaned the glasses of the spectacles with meticulously folded handkerchief, then continued with little irritation of a teacher whose simple point was not being understood by his student.

"Look Mr. Ram, I am not saying that one should not do hard work or sincere in ones duty, what I am saying is that one must also be practical".

"How can I oblige important persons, sir?" asked Ram with hesitation

"You have to find the opportunities to oblige the persons in power like your boss and seniors" replied Aroraji with a clever smile.

"Finding the opportunities?" Ram repeated the words with bewilderment

"Yes, Mr. Ram, but you need not to worry as you will learn all this with passing of time. However, as a thumb rule you must never say "NO" to your boss or any other powerful person in office" replied Aroraji with gleaming eyes and continued "what boss says or expect you must do without asking any question".

"But sir, if it is wrong or illegal" asked Ram

Aroraji thought for a while; this new chap seems to be a gone case and nothing but time can make him learn the things. It is difficult to understand how such silly person has been inducted in this reputed company.

"Mr. Ram, you must understand the difference between illegal and obligation" said Aroraji in terse voice.

Ram did not reply. 'Oblige to grow' or 'finding the opportunities to oblige' were new terminology to him.

"Sir, I am confused," said Ram in slow and depressed voice.

"Look, Mr. Ram, you are new here and have to learn a lot of new things. You have to go a long way thus learn to make the relations; and learn to oblige the persons so that you can be "rewarded" whenever an opportunity arises. See the case of Mr. Wadhava he had been nominated for foreign training just because of his contact " said Aroraji in his last ditch attempt to make him understand the practical world.

Ram remained silent, looking not to the face of Aroraji but to the floor, to his newly polished and shining shoes. He always liked the polished shoes. It was strange what little polish can do the old shoes. An old habit to look at his feet, whenever have the feelings of helplessness or disagreement. Expression of his body language when he failed to find proper words for arguments either out of respect or fear or both.

Dilemma of Ram not remained hidden from experience eyes of Aroraji. He was seeing a bleak future of this simpleton here. Instead of thanking him, instead of feeling oblige for giving such important advice, this silly chap is arguing. Wasting time for such useless person was against his rule. After all, he has some other important things to do. He had to make a lot of arrangement for boss's daughter marriage due on next week.

"Mr. Ram,I have some urgent work now. If you wish you can come some other day after giving me a ring," said Aroraji abruptly to get rid of his silly student.

Ram made a disgraceful exit from room.

Trying to seek solace in his diary, Ram wrote, "It seems that I have landed in a strange world where everyone talks about all sorts of things. Why should I say "yes" to everything of boss or do odd things to oblige people in power. If thing is not right I have full right to say ' NO'. But Aroraji said that saying no might hamper "growth". It means I have to sacrifice my freedom of saying no to move ahead.

After writing diary, Ram tried to sleep but in vain, then start reading one management book he bought recently and underlined following -

The relationship with your boss is probably the most important relationship you have at work place. Boss management can stimulate better performance; improve your working life, job satisfaction, and workload. Faster decision making and accomplishment of more – by both parties. Give your boss a hand and reap the rewards.

Ram tried to find word 'oblige' in the book but could not and satisfied Ram eventually got to sleep.

PAY & PERQUISITE

"Things that can be done in the office you need not to do at your home" advised Sailani to Mr. Ram

Ram looked blankly towards Sailani and murmured, "Yes sir"

"Things like reading news papers, magazines, asking shares rates etc and etc can be done more peacefully in the office than home" continued Sailani with evergreen smile on his big face.

Sailani, short and fat yet adding weight every year, did not mind anything if someone were ready to listen his self-written poems and philosophy. He believed in almost everything but not in doing work, of course official. Nothing could rob him from his evergreen smile

"Sir, you are only person around who looks so lively and happy" asked Ram

"Where on the earth will you be happy if not in government job?" replied Sailani with smile on his big face and continued, "In this world of uncertainty, if your pay, perks and pension is secured than what else is required to remain happy".

Ram didn't speak but nodded

"You know, I have not been promoted for last many years, may be 11 or 12 years, still I am happy and enjoying the life whereas people whose promotion is delayed even for one year crying with their lungs and dying with tension" continued Sailani with his characteristic philosophical style

"Why have you not been promoted for so long, sir?" asked Ram sympathetically.

"Because I don't practice the art of 'pleasing' the boss," answered Sailani casually and start chewing something

"Sir, I understand that boss will be pleased if we do our work sincerely and dedicatedly" said Ram, looking towards Sailani

A big laughter erupted from Sailani, shaking his bulky torso in a funny way "Mr. you are new here. I also had the same feeling when I joined." said Sailani with bitterness in his voice and stood to spit something from his mouth.

Ram was surprised by Sailani laughter. He assured himself that he didn't say anything wrong.

Sailani drank some water and continued, "Mr., as you are new here thus don't know that hard work, sincerity and such sort of things are only a desirable criterion but essential prerequisite is 'unquestioning loyalty' towards boss to remain favourite of your boss.

"Sir, it means, doing hard work has no meaning here" asked perturbed Ram

"Why not Mr. Ram, If you do the work sincerely and dedicatedly, certainly you will get the appreciation, award and, of course, more work but not necessarily reward or promotion" replied Sailani with a hidden smile on his face as if enjoying Ram's ignorance and continued "Rewards are kept reserved for obedient or loyalist"

Ram was lost and confused more than previous days. This funny looking guy was telling funny things about promotion, loyalty etc. Perhaps it was frustration of not being promoted for so long forcing him to say such depressing things. I didn't see any reason why anyone doing his duty sincerely and dedicatedly should not get his due. I myself did the hard work in my study and suitably rewarded.

Sensing Ram's dilemma over his 'reward theory' Sailani quickly added "Since you are new here thus it is too early for you to know about all these things but, you know, sometimes it is not possible to control the direction of discussion. I did not mean to discourage you but it is my duty to tell you the truth. And truth is- in Govt. Company your promotion and thus your career depends upon boss generosity over you rather than your ability, capability or workability".

Ram nodded but remained silent. In fact he was not enjoying discussion with Sailani. He was here to learn something new, some addition in his knowledge and information about office working and not for 'promotion centered' discussion.

Ignoring Ram silence, Sailani continued, albeit, with some sincerity. "Mr. Ram, you have to play a long innings here thus keep remembering one of my advice to remain happy and satisfy here – do your work with the sense of doing your duty and with the feeling of 'being paid for your time and service'. But if you are also indulged in the rat- race of 'earning' of boss's generosity in temptation of promotion and 'fringe benefit' you will also loose the comfort and privilege of being in govt. job and eventually peace of your mind".

"Sir, are you happy here i.e. being in this govt. company?" asked Ram abruptly

"As long as I am assured of getting pay and other benefits by the end of month, question of unhappiness does not arises," replied Sailaniji in his careless and casual style

"And what about career and job- satisfaction as you have not been promoted for long? asked Ram humbly

Sailani looked straight in the eyes of Ram as if he should not ask this question

"Look Mr. Ram, you may be intelligent and academically much better than me but you are far behind of me in understanding of official things. Looking for job satisfaction in Govt. Company is like pursuing mirage in desert. Thus forget everything else, do your duty and look for pay, perquisites, and then pension."

Ram said nothing

Sailaniji stood from his chair to spit out of chewed thing than continued "Mr. Ram, in job, we have to 'earn' our promotion while pay and perquisites are matter of right."

"But sir, you have some different theory about promotion something like pleasing the boss" Ram asked

“That is why I am saying we have to ‘earn’ our promotion by doing hard work as well as pleasing the boss but if someone is not interested in both i.e. neither in hard work nor in pleasing the boss, still one can remain happy and enjoy because pay and perquisites are guaranteed.”

“Does it mean that one continue to get pay even if does not do any work here” asked puzzled Ram with astonishment

Sailani drank some water from side table glass and again put up something in his mouth then spoke, “Do you know Mr. Ram, and why one get pay and other perquisites in Govt. Company?”

Ram remained silent

“We get our pay, for coming to the office not necessarily for work. If one doesn’t do any work but remain only physically presents still he / she is entitled to full pay by the end of month. Doing work in office is one’s drive of duty and conviction not a compulsion.

“And perquisite?” asked bewildered Ram

“We get perquisite for running from here to there, for pleasing undeserving and incompetent, for tolerating intolerable, for ignoring impudence of workers, for adjusting with incompatible, for tolerating nonsense and useless sermons of bosses that too with smile."

There was wild expression on Ram's face while face of Sailani was looking bright as if he had put forward some overwhelming big bang theory. It appeared that Mr. Sailani got some listener after long time for his 'belief shattering theories'.

"I know such dissection of pay & perquisite will be looking strange to you but it is a fact. And no one wants to acknowledge the facts because we all become habitual of ignoring the facts" continued Sailani

"If you have so many grudge then why you are continuing here?" asked Ram sarcastically but with humble tone

Sailani looked bitterly towards Ram and said

"You are right but I have no option but to continue this slavery as I have no other means for livelihood."

"Slavery?" asked stunned Ram

"Yes my dear, service is nothing but modern form of slavery" said Sailani with sad smile on his face and frustration in his voice.

"Sir I am not getting you, service is slavery? asked Ram with disbelief

"Yes, my dear, service is nothing but modern form of slavery" replied Sailani as if some big secret had been disclosed.

"Why are you saying so, sir?

"I am saying so because you have to come to office even if you don't have any work to do. Have to do the unproductive work you don't want to do. Have to stay in the office even if there is no work because boss is there." continued Sailani with red face

"I am saying so because you have to say YES even if you wish to say NO and have to pay the respect to those bastard who don't deserve or even don't have the worth of single penny and also have to bear the mental agony and social stigma of being left behind in the rat race of promotion, dominated by sycophants and "privileged ones' and that too after sacrificing best time of the day and prime time of your life."

"A place wherein you don't have the right to say no to no and yes to yes, a service where you have no choice but to carry out the order of less competent, less qualified but more seniors, a life where feeling of being used or ignored, cloud your creativity and ability is not lesser than paid slavery in modern form"

"And all that for few bucks and "career" continued Sailani almost out of breath "Alas! There is no exit from this slavery." Sailani body was shaking with heavy breath and he was not seeing towards Ram but towards ceiling.

After a long time 'Emotional lava' had erupted from 'frustrated volcano'

Ram was stunned with sudden outburst of Sailani.. A mix feeling of embarrassment and puzzlement was start brewing in the mind of Ram. This fat man seems to taking advantage of his being new here and thus uttering many out of context and nonsense things. There is no point of staying here and discussing anything with such a frustrated man. Frustration breeds frustration. He left the room without speaking any word.

In the evening, Ram wrote in diary

It was not important what Mr. Sailani said but the way he said was noticeable; content of his outburst may be derogatory and debatable but feeling behind it was certainly of deep frustration and helplessness of a man who had given best time of his life to the company.

How can a person be so insane to compare self with slave unless he has deep frustration towards the company?

Deep into thought, Ram took out the book and started reading about 'System and People' and wrote underline portion of it in his diary

'What really matter for a company or organization is system as well as people; none can work in isolation, as both should be complimentary to each other for progress of organization.

The employee commitment to its company depend upon

1. *Individual traits, his/ her capabilities, attitude and particularly values*
2. *Organization's treatment, type of boss and award /punishment system.*

Perhaps Sailaniji had not been given proper or deserving treatment by the company either by its policy or boss, resulting caustic feeling in him and subsequent cascading impact on his career. Perhaps it is insanity of Mr. Sailani who has brought him to this type of frustration to compare self with slave.

Still Salani words “Alas! There is no exit from this slavery.” is ringing in my ear. I do not know what I should do. If I believe what Sailani said then I must run away from here. But, where? Is it easy to get the job?

EXCELLENT SUBORDINATE

After reaching office, offering prayer for 2-3 minutes to various Gods, placed under glass of table top, then started reading the folded newspaper for half an hour was daily ritual of Vermaji before starting the 'official ritual'.

Having different rings in all the fingers of right hand- five fingers, five rings. All rings were having different color of something called stones. As rings were not sufficient Vermaji also wore some metallic band in his hand – overall giving the feeling of some land lord instead of bureaucrat. It seems he wished to control all the nature -power by wearing different rings. Believing lesser in self but much more in God..

Vermaji, a born 'job evader', hated doing the job (of course official) himself. Monitoring others, finding faults in their jobs and exaggerate them at all available occasions was his favorite choice of passing the time in office. He himself never did the job of any worth but did the post-mortem of jobs of others wholeheartedly as if an expert of all things.

He never took the decision of any value himself but severely criticized decisions of others.

Making mess of simple things, igniting spark and enjoying the fire and other similar sort of things were others areas of his interests.

Vermaji's agenda was very clear - *avoid the job but appease the boss.*

He was deeply engrossed in the last page of newspaper when telephone ring broke his attention. He gave telephone a hatred look. He never liked the telephone because it either informed about boss's summons or subordinates' problems.

And Vermaji hated both.

Phone continued to ring. Vermaji never picked up telephone before 4th ring.

In his view, it had two advantages -first it gave the impression to caller that he was busy and second one, more important than first, -if message was not important or urgent then telephone-caller will cut off its own after 3rd or 4th ring without giving him any trouble. After all, to look busy was a valuable survival skill.

So Vermaji waited up to 4th ring of telephone with mental calculation about whose call it may be at this unusual point of time i.e so early. Eventually he picked up the phone.

"Why do you take such a long time to pick up the phone?" inquired the boss with unpleasant voice

Tone of boss was showing some urgency and experienced Vermaji thought it prudent not to utter anything except 'yes sir'

"Project meeting is at 11 am in conference hall. Bring the project report" ordered the boss in hurried voice before snapping the call.

Vermaji, quick to understand what others, particularly, boss want, was stunned for a while with the unusual desperation and irritation in his boss's voice. His analytical and experienced mind understood two- three points quickly

First –boss had been fired either by big- boss or some other big one thus had to be avoided for some time. Second – meeting was urgent one as it would be chaired by big- boss (venue and timing of meeting was enough to give this indication). Lastly, project report was needed probably to convince the big boss about progress of the work. After all written things make better impression than spoken ones in such matter.

But, unfortunately, project report was not ready yet as it was not updated after last meeting. 'This is not my fault, whispered Vermaji to self, after all such reports are usually updated 1-2 days before meeting and this meeting was scheduled to be held in next week, what I can do, if meeting is being held before schedule date and that too without prior information'. Vermaji was perturbed and at a loss over this unexpected development.

Telling to boss, at this point of time, that report was not ready or giving justification about it would certainly raise boss's temperature as boss himself was in tension of meeting with big boss. Making boss angry during this period of filling of annual confidential report would be suicidal.

'Something has to be done' he whispered to self with a glance on his gold plated wrist watch. He gave a thought to the situation and his options. Existing old project report cannot be modified in such a short time. Boss can't be told about the fact that report was not ready. Vermaji felt himself in a fix for few moments. Suddenly idea flashed to his shrewd mind - to give the fresh printout of the old report of last meeting. He knew very well that usually no one read the report in meeting. But if boss detected that report was not modified. Vermaji thought for a while and then relaxed. If this happened, blame can be put on computer Virus. Everyone knew about virus and nasty things it could do to the computer and its contents.

Moreover, this option of giving old report in new print out was certainly better choice at this point of time than telling boss that report was not ready.

Vermaji started taking print out of the old report on fresh crisp -white papers with relaxed mood, singing an old song on the tune of whistle. He was not in hurry, after all new print out of old report must not be given to boss before 11 a.m. so that boss would not get the time to read it.

Vermaji was in pensive mood and thinking, "Life is not about right or wrong but choosing the best among available options."

Like

- Choosing one-eyed among blinds.
- Giving new print out of the old report than saying no to boss.

"Good morning sir," said Ram in his typical style as he entered in the room.

Vermaji raised his head, saw Ram but said nothing and again became busy in shuffling of recently taken print out of the report. He was in no mood to entertain anyone at this point of time. “I am busy in preparing an important report you may come afterwards” said Vermaji casually

As Ram had nothing to do and nowhere to go except to be associated with Vermaji for his ongoing familiarization training thus spoke politely to Vermaji

“Sir, should I help you in taking the print out”

Vermaji gave a hard look to Ram but said nothing, thought for a moment, then beckoned him to sit at nearby chair and continued checking of the fresh print out. Still there are 35 minutes left in 11 am, He had already informed to boss that report was ready but print out being delayed due to some printer problem.

“Yes, what I can do for you Mr.?” said Vermaji, relaxing himself in the chair.

“Sir, my name is Ram and I am new appointee here and want to be benefited from your vast experience as part of my familiarization programme” said Ram in almost one breath in robotic tone as he had repeated this sentence many times since his joining.

Vermaji gave him another hard look and remain silent. 'Why should I share my experience for the benefit of others? This world is driven by the philosophy of give and take and this new one cannot give me any thing of my benefit thus why should I enrich him from my experience of 25 years?' thought Vermaji

Ram was not perturbed with the silence and hard look of Vermaji. In fact he had learned that such people gave more valuable advices than other vocal ones, if persuaded well.

"Sir, you are having valuable experience of years and certainly your advice can benefit a novice like me" pleaded Ram with all innocence on his face.

Usually words do not impress Vermaji but it was the innocence on Ram's face and pleading in his voice that impressed him slightly. In past, during his initial years of service, he worked a lot and also suffered a lot but gradually he learned the rule of games and then suffered little as worked little.

"Sir, please, I will be obliged" these words from Ram was sufficient enough to drive the last nail in Vermaji's inflated ego.

"Yes, Mr Ram, what do you want from me?" asked Vermaji.

Ram thought for a while then asked *"What makes one an excellent subordinate*?"

Vermaji smiled a bit and appreciated the boy for picking up the topic of his choice and said "In *corporate world,* govt. organization in particular, no one is an absolute boss. Everyone is subordinate of someone in hierarchy. It is not difficult to be a good boss but it is certainly difficult to be a good subordinate of someone in power. Many times good bosses do fail as subordinates to their bosses". Vermaji continued after having a look on his wrist watch –*"Good* subordination is an art and like any other arts it needs creative thinking. Hard work, good efficiency, never saying NO etc alone do not necessarily make someone good or excellent subordinate. Success of a subordinate depends on the fact whether he or she also be able to extract out maximum from their boss or not. If you are good on both count i.e in your work as well as in extracting out maximum from boss then you are an excellent subordinates."

"Extracting maximum from boss?" repeated Ram with amazement on his face and surprise in his eyes. He recently read about managing your boss in the book but extracting maximum from boss was new terminology to him.

"Yes, If you remember and follow the following rules."

RULE 1 SHOW YOUR BOSS YOU BELONG TO HIM

"As a subordinate you are a proprietary item of your boss. Every boss thinks that he has bona fide right over his subordinates. To win the favor of your boss, as a subordinate, it is your duty to keep reinforcing this belief or illusion of the boss that *you belong to him i.e. you are 100% loyal to him* " continued experienced one, after drinking some water, with serious note in his voice that made Ram also serious.

"Mr, Ram, remember, simply being good and hardworking is not enough if you fails on the count of 'belongingness' or loyalty in boss's eyes. It is a must thing while others qualities are desirable. It can be simply understood by the fact that no matter how strong is door but if its locking system is not good, it is of no use."

"Sir, I am confused how door and lock is concerned with all this?" Ram said impatiently

Vermaji smiled and replied

Mr. Ram, locking system is analogous to loyalty while door to quality of person. Thus if one want to extract maximum from boss one must not failed on this count.

"What should be done for this" asked novice

"You must remember the following to show your boss that you belong to him"

a) Never dares to bypass your boss

'Some over enthusiastic or over -smart subordinates do the mistakes of giving the information clandestinely to big boss or to the boss of their own bosses to get importance and to fulfill vested interests. This is very dangerous game in which, sooner or later, subordinate end up as a bigger looser.

b) Avoid to be seen with the person whom your boss feel his competitor or do not like

'Mr. Ram, bureaucracy is the game of power and position. Every one of us directly or indirectly plays or become part of power game to win or have upper hand in rat-race. Higher one goes more deeply one indulged in the power game. And more deeply one indulged in power game more insecure he / she become. In power- matter, boss is always on higher echelon than his subordinates thus his insecurity level is also remain higher. It is possessive mentality of bosses towards their subordinates as well as their insecurity that can cast shadow on subordinate career if one continue to be seen with opposite camp. Remember, Mr. Ram, any boss can adjust his subordinates incompetency but not his disloyalty. Instead of a competent but disloyal he will prefer to have incapable but loyal subordinate.'

c) Do not keep your boss in pitch dark,

'In today's age, information is power. Apart from content of information, it also matter from where or whom you get it. Subordinates usually exaggerate good news but hide bad news from boss. And one fine morning, boss is caught by surprise when this bad news comes to his knowledge from third party. This shake up not only his confidence but trust also in the subordinate."

"At work place, boss- subordinate relationship is not only about work but also about loyalty, trust, confidence and respect. Thus don't keep boss in pitch dark about bad news. Illuminate him with 'fact line' if not 'paragraph' about bad news also so that his trust on you remain intact. Remember shaken confidence about someone capability may be restored but not the shaken trust."

Ram was overwhelmed not only with the content and clarity of Vermaji but the way of its delivery. He was thinking how wrong sometimes we go in judging the people from their outer appearance. His impression about Vermaji was changing for better with passing of each minute.'

RULE 2 KEEP TELLING BOSS THAT HE IS RIGHT

"Don't try to argue with your boss" said old one

"But if I feel I am right" asked new one

"Mr. Ram, it is not the question of right or wrong but of whom you are speaking to or rather of question of ego. And certainly ego of boss has to be in higher echelon than yours. Unfortunately when we try to convince or argue someone, we unknowingly raise level of our ego to prove rightness of our point and thus malign others ego. Thus argument or such sorts of things are with same level or peers but not with someone in power".

"What should I do or say if I am convince that my point is right" asked perturbed Ram

"Mr. Ram, in the matter of boss and subordinate, boss is always right. Thus even if you feel you are right then keep telling boss "You are very right, sir but alternately it can be this way or that way also". Mr. Ram, barring few exception, boss understand quickly what subordinate wants or talking about but it is his 'boss ego' that stop him admitting it that his knowledge or understanding of the issue is lesser than subordinates. So first inflate ego of your boss then get what you want from him. Remember, as a thumb rule, argument with powerful, ignorant and your spouse always have disastrous outcome, no matter how wrong are they or how right are you".

Rule 3 Speak what boss want to listen

"A good subordinate should tell only those things to boss that he wants to listen."

"It means we should not tell the fact to boss if it is bitter, " asked new one

"Inform him about facts but don't discuss it"

"But both informing and telling are same"

"No, informing has official touch while telling is personal. While informing is a line, telling or discussing is like paragraph. Fact has to be told to boss to protect your integrity but don't tell the truth behind it if it does not please the boss ears. As we prefer some butter over plain bread to please our taste buds similarly avoid plain speaking to boss. Do some sugar coating on facts before telling to boss. It helps him in 'digesting" them.

Rule 4 Look busy and concerned

"As parents feels satisfied whenever they saw their children are reading, even if they are not reading. Similarly boss or seniors feel satisfied if their juniors are busy. In govt. jobs it is not the output that matter much but looking busy and concerned certainly pays you. Thus whenever you go to the boss room you should have 2-3 files with you. Look little bit in hurry as you have other jobs to finish. Show concerned about other jobs also which are not related to you. In nut shell give impression of 'loaded with work' to boss. Looking busy and concerned is a valuable survival skill. Human being is strange creature – it enjoy seeing others out of comfort i.e other comfort make them uncomfortable. And if this human being is your boss or seniors vested with some power over you than they feel it their birth right to bring you out of comfort i.e giving some extra or odds jobs to you. Thus remember one saying in Hindi

Kam na kar, per kam ki phikar jarur kar

Kam ki phikar na bhi kar, per kam ka jikar jarur kar

(Don't do the work but must show your concerned about work; even if you don't show concerned still ask about the status of work)

With these words Vermaji stand up to leave the room as it is about 11 am, time to give the report to boss, crisp print out, old wine in new bottle. NO in the bottle of YES.

Ram was not able to sleep even though he was in bed for more than one hour. Vermaji advice made him more confused. He wondered whether he would ever be able to match the 'talents' of persons like Vermaji, Mishraji or Aroraji

He got up and wrote in diary

'Perhaps the biggest folly of God is the creation of human beings and his desire to control or rule over own species. How a human being rule over others? How's that one should not say no to another human being because he or she is in power?. Right and wrong does not matter but boss matter, pleasing of boss supersede question of right or wrong. What a pity it is.'

To quench his mental faculty, Ram reach out for one management book and underlined following

There are three kinds of employees in any organization

1. *Good for nothing -Those who cannot do even their current job right*

2. *Good for repetitive job- Those who can do their current job but not capable of further growth. These high input but low output types don't have any aptitude for new learning; simply by repetition they can do their current job satisfactorily. But never look beyond that*

3. *Good for everything – highly adaptive, and ready to take additional responsibilities and deserve high growth and are real asset to any company*

The irony of the govt. office is that 'Good for nothing' type become loyal to boss, doing all odds jobs of boss without any iota of grudge and thus get good confidential report and thus promotion as well as 'fringe benefits' like training, tour etc

'Good for repetitive jobs' type also gets the attention of boss as they always comes when boss calls and remain busy and do the jobs like ants.

And third ones-'Good for everything', barring a few lucky ones , gets frustrated with boss, stifling bureaucratic system and non -intellectual activities . Some daring one left the comfort and security of govt. company and ventured out in private company while others keep on rotting, rusting and cursing there doing odd jobs and start indulging in dirty office politics that further worsen their frustration. Eventually company left with type one and type two and frustrated ones of type three.

Ram tried to figure out Vermaji's category in vain and finally slept.

X FACTOR

The atmosphere of the boss's room was gloomy.

Boss was sad. Thus his 'trusted' subordinates had to be looked sad even if they did not feel so.

Reason?

Boss did not get the promotion.

A shock to Prasadji, the born boss

A surprise to subordinates. After all, Prasadji had impeccable record of managing his all promotion so far.

The gloomy atmosphere of the boss's office was of defeated ruling party, where leader and his trusted stalwarts were assembled for retrospection after an unexpected defeat.

Prasadji, had yet to come out from the shock. Embarrassment of not being promoted was a new experience to him. Almost oblivious of subordinates' presence, Prasadji, was deep in thought. What went wrong? His contacts in Head Quarter had assured him thus he was confident to get the promotion this time also.

But something went wrong. Not only went wrong but also added salt to his injury as his old colleague and arch rival Chandra had been promoted.

Apart from shock and embarrassment of not being promoted, promotion of his rival Chandra, had made things more complicated and difficult for him. Prasadji's shrewd and calculating mind started troubling him for coming days. Deep in thought, he murmured

'Would it be easy to work under Chandra, his colleague till yesterday, but his boss henceforth?'

'Would it be easy to tell wife and children that car and other 'facilities' are no longer in his control and he has to depend on bastard Chandra, who must have used some political influence to get the promotion?'

Prasadji was used to of the 'reward' associated with promotion but never before tasted the 'stigma' of not being promoted. He wiped his face and took water from one of two glass kept on his big size table before falling again in pensive mode with perturbed mind. Never before in his service life he felt so low. Till yesterday his power was Teflon coated, as he was in good book of everyone. After all he took care of everyone, he obliged everyone -but now on --. He knew very well that in bureaucracy power was everything and power come with promotion. Each promotion means- more power, more opportunities and more contacts.

'Sinking feeling' was engulfing him.

Subordinates were also thinking, albeit with little sadness in their heart but more on faces.

"Boss deserves this; last time I did not get the promotion because of him. Bastard spoiled my performance report. It is soothing to see him feeling the heat" one of second rung subordinate was thinking with artificial sadness on his face but music in his heart.

"Subordinates growth depends upon boss growths and if boss did not get promotion how shall I? After all one should not expect generous performance report or other fringe benefits from a loser," subordinate no 1, closest to boss, was thinking.

"I have to find some other influential person than Prasadji. There is no point worshipping the 'looser- boss' any more. One who can't manage his own promotion in HQ how he will manage my transfer and posting" another 'loyalist', desperate for transfer at his hometown, was thinking.

After long silence, most confidant subordinate of boss said, "Sir, this new Chairman will ruin the company. If he don't reward person like you then how this company will survive".

Others also nodded in sympathy.

Boss didn't say anything but looked towards roof. Balm of sympathy was perhaps enough to sooth the 'injury' of not being promoted but not enough to sooth the 'wound' of Chandra's promotion. Even thinking of prospect of working under Chandra was insulting and disgusting. But in bureaucracy, one has limited choice or rather no choice.

And, when everyone in the room was thinking and air was gloomy, Mr. Ram entered in the Prasadji's office as a part of his familiarization training.

"Good morning to Sir, and to everyone" said Ram in cheerful tone

Boss gave the reply from his gloomy eyes

Subordinates looked towards him with questions.

Ram remained in standing position for few seconds waiting for signal to seat.

His sixth sense told him that something was wrong

"Is everything all right" Ram asked in whispered voice as he managed to sit down nearby to an accommodating subordinate.

"Boss did not get the promotion" whispered the subordinate

"Why did boss not get the promotion? asked inquisitive Ram with childish look on his face and question mark in his eyes

Subordinate didn't reply.

Boss also didn't reply. In fact he wished that someone should throw this newcomer idiot out from the room. His mood was very much upset and he wished to be left alone for some time.

Ram was about to ask another question but thought it prudent to remain silent. Experience of previous days, particularly with Pandeyji, was still looming large in his mind. Ram had now become little bit conscious in asking questions, particularly to powerful persons. Although so many questions were coming to his analytical mind but he preferred to remain silent at the moment and thought it wise to ask them at proper time with the proper person, not having teeth to bite.

Thirst has to be quenched, no matter where from water come.

Understanding the situation and mood of boss, most confident, senior most subordinate thought it prudent to leave the boss alone. He beckoned to other subordinates. After all, funeral procession should not stay long enough at graveyard. Moreover they have to congratulate Chandra Sahab'.

Chandra Sahab, new boss, new power- center and new hope for the opportunists.

"Please tell me why Chandraji got the promotion and Prasadji didn't" asked Ram from confident subordinate no 1 of Prasadji in the canteen.

Confident subordinate, most senior among the battalion of subordinates, did not answer. In fact his mind was preoccupied in firming up of strategy to become confident of Chandra Sahab, who is bound to become in charge, after this unexpected development.

"After all I am due to promotion next year and without becoming confident of Chandraji it won't be possible" murmured most confident subordinate to self. "No doubt Prasadji was good to me, but now in this changed scenario continuation of goodness of Prasadji was doubtful. A looser can't be generous to others. Be with winner, if you also want to be winner. Till now Prasadji was winner and my impeccable loyalty was with him but-----. Next promotion is very important for my career -- In today cut throat competition I can't take the risk. I have to change-----------"

"Please tell me why Chandraji got the promotion and Prasadji not? Was Chandraji doing more job or more efficient than Prasadji" Ram's child –like insistence broke the stream of thought of the senior most subordinate, named Jain.

"Mr Ram you are new here thus won't understand certain things; you will learn such things with passing of time "replied Jain dryly to get rid of him.

"But, Sir, I want to learn the things as fast as possible and sir, if you help me, I will be highly obliged" said Ram with request filled eyes

"Sir" that is the word that always pleased Jain. As soon as his ear listen musical word "sir" feeling of importance dawn over him and his desire of becoming very big when many people, including his colleague, will address him as Sir became young.

A small desire in the heart of big opportunist

"Sir, please, I will be obliged" continued Ram. This was sufficient enough to drive nail in inflated ego of Jain.

"Mr.Ram, Chandraji got the promotion because he has better contacts in HQ"

"But sir, promotion should be linked with our work, our performance and experience" asked curious Ram

"This world is not driven by 'should' or 'shouldn't' but by give and take" said Jain philosophically, and continued "Mr. Ram, getting promotion depends on many factors. Simply being efficient or hard working does not entitle someone for promotion"

"What are these factors, sir"

"Though there are many factors, which you will learn over period of time, but most important is X factor to influence promotion" said Jain in a low but authoritative voice

It always gives him immense pleasure to talk someone with authority.

"X factor, what is it, sir ?" asked puzzled Ram

"X factor is the essence of everything," replied Jain in philosophical voice and continued "One who understood this X factor will always remain in winning position"

"Sir, I am not getting you"

"To understand X factor it is better to comprehend this example -Suppose you have three sons, and one of them do nothing but study all the day and also get good mark. Second son remain busy in playing all the day resulting poor performance in study; while third son excel not only in his exam but also in games and other extra-curricular activities"

"Which son would be your favorite ?" asked Jain with glow in his eyes

"Obviously third one who is good in study as well as in games and other activities" answered Ram in a confused voice

"Similarly only by doing hard work in office you can't become hot favorite of boss; you must also be good in "other activities" of boss's liking.

X factor was a new terminology for Ram. He was wondering how fast he was learning new "things". In his academic career whatever he learnt that was chiefly through book and teachers but here everybody is like an island in himself. How different is life and people here.

“What should I do to get X factor?” asked new one

“You should not question what boss says or ordered” advised the old one

“If, what boss says is not logical” asked confused one

“When boss says something, question of logic or ill -logic does not arise but of following it” continued the experienced one

“It means hard work and dedication towards works has nothing to do with promotion” asked the curious one

“Hard work and dedication is desirable and prerequisite but not the essential criteria for promotion “said old one” while obeying the boss without asking any question is the essential criteria. By simply doing outstanding job you can’t get outstanding performance report, some X factor is also needed along with work to be outstanding. And this X factor is none but boss. If your boss is pleased with you this X factor will be in your favors”.

“But, if what boss says is not in the interest of the Company?”

“Mr. Ram learn to protect your interest first. And your interest is safeguarded only if you follow and take care of boss." advised wiser one before standing up.

New man learned the new lesson.

Ram highlighted following in recently bought management book

If you put a donkey in the company of horses, of course donkey will not become horse but over period of time donkey start feeling and behaving like horse and eventually ended up neither donkey nor horse. Similarly in corporate world, particularly in In Govt. Company some born incompetent persons revolve around competent ones, keep them happy by doing their even and odd jobs and thus remain in prominence. With time these incompetent ones also start feeling and behaving as competent ones and eventually expose their real worth.

SECRET OF CALMNESS

"Sir, how do you remain so happy and calm?" asked Ram

Purohitji smiled but spoke nothing and continued to browse a file.

"Sir, here I observed, everyone seems to be in tension and harbor some grudge against others" continued Ram, sitting in front of veteran Purohitji, on the sixth day of his familiarization program.

Short, overweight, always smiling and calm, Purohitji had very charming and friendly smile that makes other person instantly comfortable. No one ever saw him in hurry or in tension. Even if sky falls or earthquake come, Purohitji remained cool. Always doing something, never keeping any grudge against anyone be it boss, peers or subordinates. Purohitji was an epitome of equanimity.

Ram waited for a while for response, and then said, "Sir I want to learn secret of your calmness"

"Human being rarely learn anything from preaching or advice but from own mistakes and experiences," replied Purohitji calmly without raising his head from file.

'Sir, I will be obliged if you kindly give me some advice on maintaining calmness even in adversity."

"Look, Mr. Ram, as you are new here, thus will not be able to comprehend and appreciate many things. Moreover, impact of preaching or advice does not have lasting impact thus hardly add any enduring value to listener" replied Purohitji in his characteristic philosophical and smiling style as if some religious guru delivering sermon to his audience.

It did not take Ram much time to understand that behind outer politeness of Purohitji inside lies not easy to crack toughness. But till now he had understood the power of gentle persuasions to crack the inflated ego of senior and powerful persons.

"Sir, you are right, a novice like me, may not be able to fully comprehend advices of knowledgeable person like you, still I am sincerely interested to listen you " pleaded Ram not only with words but also from his body language

Purohitji, looked at the face of Ram- simple, over enthusiastic to learn the things. This boy was bound to suffer in this jungle of civilized animals. Purohitji thought for a while and then said

"Look, Mr. Ram, it is all in mind. It is mind that troubles us more than our body. All feelings originate in mind and our body is simply an extension of mind to express those feeling. Among all feelings that originate in mind, fear of losing what we have and desire for more moves this world. Secret of calmness lies in overcoming both i.e. fear of losing and desire for more." whispered Purohitji in mediated voice.

"Fear of losing? I didn't get it, sir" said Ram in confused voice.

Purohitji paused for some time then continued, "Mr. Ram, our work place is our karam –bhoomi, our battle –ground where everyone has to play a certain role and duty to do. Instead of doing our job as duty, *as depicted in Gita, we* generally do our job to please those who matters, either by doing extra hard works or by unnecessary flattery or both in hope of getting some reward in future as well as in fear of losing comfort or status of our present position"

"Right sir" replied Ram

"This hope, of getting some better position in future and fear of losing or worsening whatever we have in present, *not only* keep us tense *but also* rob us from enjoying whatever we have. More hope and fear, more tension of pleasing and performing and eventually people enter in a vicious circle" Purhoitji paused for few minutes to take water and then continued, "Thus if you can resist the 'carrot' and brave the 'fear baton' only then you will be able to enjoy eternal calmness in bureaucratic system of govt. company."

"But sir, hope or desire of getting better or more and fear of losing or worsening the present position are innate feeling of human being and thus cannot be overcome" said perplexed Ram

Purohitji looked the boy with appreciation and replied,

"You are right Mr. Ram these are innate things of human being and thus difficult to overcome but keeping them in control is in our hand. This controlling add some more worth in our life instead of entering in rat race". said Purohitji and then continued after a short pause

"Mr. Ram it has to be clearly understood that what should be our driving force at work place–satisfaction of doing our duty honestly and dedicatedly or tension of doing for pleasing others. People waste their energy, time and peace either in the hope of carrot or fear of baton but hardly they get any and even if they get it that make their life more tensed. You take the case of Mr. Mandal. He does not have his own life. His weekends are on the mercy of his boss. He run post to pillars lesser for the work but more to please his boss. He works like a donkey and behave like a monkey in the hope of carrot and for fear of baton."

"But sir, here everyone talk about pleasing the boss and advised never say no to boss and all this sort of things if one want to grow. You are only one who is telling just opposites. Will it not make bosses feel offended If one don't care to please or fear them?"

Purohitji smiled and said nothing for few minutes then spoke" Mr. Ram, when you came in my office you asked me that how do I remained so happy and calm while everyone seems tense."

"Yes sir" replied subdued Ram.

"My driving force at work place is my sense of duty and performing it with best of my abilities and intentions. I give full regards to boss, to seniors and to deserving ones also but I don't get my salary to please them thus I do my job without caring the carrot and fearing the baton and I am satisfied and happy."

Ram remained silent he was utterly confused. He didn't know what to learn and what not.

Sensing his dilemma, Purohitji continued "Mr. Ram, you are young and have a long way to go. You have to decide your direction. If you want to have calmness of mind and satisfaction of doing you have to ever remember following, if not then dumped them after going out from my room".

1. Instead of carrot, make your duty your driving force.

2. Prefer losing instead of compromising your conscience.

3. Have the due respect for boss and seniors but don't grant them your permission to use you as per their wish and take you granted.

4. Don't compare. There is no end of rat race in bureaucracy. In this world nothing comes free. Probably, people who have gone ahead of you, must have lost many other things in the process. There are plenty more important things in life than your career.

5. Be humble and be human as humility + humanity increase face values of *our* other good qualities as well as diminish impact of negatives in us.

"Mr. Ram, in today fast changing world good human beings is being fast replaced by good human machines i.e human without compassions or emotions, to be successful in the world. Surely one will get much success by becoming human machine in materialistic world but not the calmness of mind.

This is all what I knew and learned from life so far. Here I am playing slog over of my career while you have full innings ahead. You yourself have to decide your course of life based on the experience of others and your internal calling". advised Purhoitji

There was silence after sermon.

Purohitji was looking exhausted after delivering his sermon

Ram was looking confused after listening sermon.

And it was the ringing of telephone that broke the silence.

Purohitji allowed it to ring for some more time before attending it.

"You can come any other time, Mr. Ram, if you desire so" said Purohitji with his characteristic charming smile and start searching some papers.

Ram left the room, more confused, then yesterday.

MAN FROM HEAD - QUARTER

He was transferred from Head Quarter. All rules, regulations, circulars, & office order were known to this 'HQ man'. Not only known, how to bend them or find the by -pass was also clear to him. The man from HQ was instant hit in the project office.

Man from HQ was 'signature fancy' i.e. believed in taking signatures of maximum people on any proposal.

"More signatures, particularly of seniors' persons, on any file- more safe are you. After all, there is no punishment for collective mistakes or failure in bureaucracy." he used to tell to his colleagues. Instead of finding the ways to get the job done he find the rules and ways to take the signature of maximum persons on any damn proposal & paper and not mind to stall the things in want of it.

Another area of his expertise was to get the thing delayed without taking any blame on him. Sending the file to other section or person on last working day of week that too at the fag- end of the day was one of his favorite skills to put the blame on other shoulders. Record keeping of dates and time of any file and paper movement etc in his diary was meticulous.

As Ram entered in the room of 'HQ man ', high decibel discussion was in progress between him and one of his subordinate.

"I don't know how you are doing works here; you are not following any rules religiously" said the HQ man in annoyed voice

"But sir, if this irrelevant, age old rule is followed 'religiously' the job will not finish in time and company may incur serious financial loss" replied subordinate who was vastly experienced in doing work efficiently, dedicatedly and honestly. He believed in finding the ways to expedite the works. His main concern was progress of the work and benefit of the company and for it he didn't mind removing or lowering superfluous hurdles to expedite the work.

"Whatever written has to be followed word by word" continued HQ man keeping stress on 'word by word'.

For HQ man, rules were priority not the work, strict observance of written words not the sprit behind it. He didn't mind to crucify the work for a small written word. For him Grammar is important not the meaning of sentence.

"But sir, it is impractical and will seriously hamper progress of work resulting loss to the Company" replied subordinate in worried voice

"That I don't know" replied HQ man casually as if work, progress were strange terms to him.

As if Geology things to Mathematics student.

"But sir, we are being paid to see the interest of the Company." protested subordinate

"But I can't jeopardize my interest in zeal of protecting interest of the Company" said HQ man curtly

"By doing right things how we can jeopardize our interest?."

"Mr. Sharma what did you get by protecting the interest of Company -vigilance and audit. And you have been not promoted for last so many years because of these" said HQ man in sarcastic voice and continued "Sharmaji you have longer service than me but it seems you have not learnt your lesson well – *don't burn your finger to poke the fire.*"

Subdued subordinate, Sharma, left the room with redness on face and as if someone had slapped him. He had sadness in his eyes and bitterness in his heart. He was brave enough to endure any inquiry or vigilance because he knew he had not done anything materialistic wrong. Some procedural wrong might had happen during process of doing things. But stigma associated with 'vigilance' and doubting eyes of colleagues or seniors humiliated him deep enough. Sometime he wonders what for he was being punished. Instead of rewarding, he was being victimized for expediting the things. According to him true job of vigilance was to punish those who delayed the things on flimsy ground and on account of absurd rules causing not only loss to the Company but also 'lost opportunities'. Such hurdle creators, strict rules compliant were causing more damage to company rather than those who performed faster and in the process didn't mind to bend the rules. Rules come after the Company not before Company. And if any rules stop us for benefitting the Company then there was nothing wrong in overruling it. After all we get our bread and butter from the Company and it was our duty to see the welfare of our bread –butter giver.

But sadly there was no punishment, no vigilance for non-performing. It was only performer or doer of things who face the heat of inquiry & vigilance.

More sadly and deeply hurting was that no one stands in favor of you or even sympathizes.

Sharma wondered who would work and think for the Company under such 'vigilant' atmosphere. People need to be trusted if system entrusted responsibility and power to them.

"People don't learn the lesson even after burning their fingers," murmured HQ man.

"Yes sir," replied Ram, sitting in front of HQ man

"What for you have come to me?"

"Sir, I am new appointee in the Company and trying to learn-------"

"Do you have any office order to come to me?" interrupted HQ man

"Sir, I have been put under familiarization training. Today I was supposed to report Srivastavaji but he was on leave. I thought I should be benefited from your experience as you are from HQ," said Ram with best possible politeness in his voice

HQ man thought for a while. As such he has nothing in writing about this chap thus not bound to entertain him and could say no to him. But as nothing to do and nowhere to go and nothing to give in writing to this chap he thought to chat with the young man.

"Though I have lot of things to do yet I don't want to disappoint you and can share my experience" said HQ man, stretching both hands above his head, pushing chair back.

"People around say that you are expert in rules and regulations" asked Ram

"You know, earlier I was in HQ and worked there for 15 years. Experience of HQ was invaluable" said HQ man with pride and gleam in his eyes.

"But sir, here, it is general belief that you do big talk about rules but little about work"

"People who say all this bullshit are idiots of first category" said HQ man with angered filled eyes and continued "rules are made to follow. Doing work without observance of rules is like cutting tree branch while sitting on it. No one reward you if everything goes well but everyone will be out to hang you if something goes wrong during work. Thus don't sacrifice your career in the enthusiasm of doing work or your duty without observance of rules" advised HQ man to learner

"But not doing work in fear of 'if something happened wrong' is also not acceptable. After all we are being paid for doing the work" said unconvinced Ram.

"Who is saying not to do the work? What I am saying compromising rules for the sake of work is not acceptable and not good for career"

"If rules are hindrance in delivering desired output why it can't be modified or best abolished" asked Ram.

"Rules are meant to fix the responsibilities or to find the scapegoat if something goes wrong in the Company interest and statutory matter. And if you don't want to be scapegoat then follow the rules word by word first then think about work. This is my plain advice to you Mr. Ram" warned HQ man

There was long silence between HQ man and novice.

Novice was finding it difficult to digest logics of HQ man.

HQ man was finding it difficult to continue discussion with novice.

After all how long a primary and a degree student could continue discussion.

Later in the evening, Ram was reading an interesting story about some important job that was completed and being inaugurated by some big boss. Ram underlined the following from the story

'Everyone was falling over each other's to take the credit and prove his competence to boss. Real mover and doer of the thing, who shed their sweat in doing the things, had been pushed far behind in the crowd of credit takers. No one wants to left behind. Everyone was uttering nice things and contributions they made in success of the things. There are also many ones who till yesterday were not even aware of the A B C of things but are in the front row of credit takers, trying to explain the things with utmost sincerity. Coconuts were being broken by all those who mattered.

Suddenly, unexpectedly, something bizarre things happened. As soon as inauguration button was pushed by big-boss things fell apart with a thud and dust along with sound of clapping, as if resonance of clapping brought down the things. Everyone was surprised and shocked and wondering what happened. Within few minutes, front runners in credit- takers, evaporated as dew in sun. And left no one but real doer of the work to understand and analyzed what went wrong and to take the blame and feel the heat of failure and inquiry. Truly said "success has many fathers but failure is orphan"

ADVICES OF WISE OLD MAN

"Learn to stir the milk to get butter out of it," advised wise old man to new man.

"But sir, I understand this company is not in the business of milk & butter" said Ram with childish look on his face

Is this new chap a simpleton? Old man thought for a moment then continued with irritation in his voice

"Mr. I didn't mean real butter or milk. I was simply quoting a proverb to emphasize my point"

Ram looked blankly towards old man. He cursed self for making his poor impression by not understanding simple thing and spoke apologetically

"Sir, I am new and inexperienced, thus could not get your point. I will be obliged if you kindly enlighten me by elaborating it".

Old man, joined the company long back on a junior post in very young age and learnt the lessons of life quickly and grew handsomely due to his quick wit, hard work and boldness. He shed his all hairs very early and thus nicknamed 'old man' from very beginning. He was brilliant –analyst, hard core opportunist as well as tough nut to crack. Subordinates regarded him, peers liked him, and boss feared him. That awesome clout he enjoyed in his heydays. Now, at the fag- end of his illustrious career, when he really became old, he had left with none but some retrospection and introspection as he was going to superannuate next month.

Old man saw the new incumbent closely, thought for few moments but said nothing. He remembered the days when he was young like this boy and joined the company.

"Sir, I will be thankful and obliged" said Ram politely

Nothing melts an old man so quickly as regard and politeness from younger one s

Old man started chewing something like tobacco and then after a long pause started.

"Look Mr. Ram, you are new here and will learn everything, if you really intend to learn. Here, in the company many persons work but only few of them remain in lime -light while others remain unnoticeable even though they do more work then lime- lighted ones. If you want to remain in later category then you need not to learn anything and simply keep on getting the salary by the end of month and forget the world. But if you have the desire in the heart and fire in the belly to be among front runner, then learn creating and encashing the opportunity" said the old man in mysterious voice coming out from deep experience well of 37 years.

"Creating and encashing the opportunities?" asked bewildered Ram

First this milk- butter theory and now this creating and encashing the opportunities. Ram was at his wits end.

"Yes, Mr. Ram, because there are always three ways of handling any problem first – ignore it, second- take immediate action and third one is allow it to snowball it then take the credit of solving it. Thus opportunity can be created if one remain vigilant and act with prudent planning in the bureaucratic system"

Ram was silent. In fact he was at loss and not able to understand what Old Man was saying. Suddenly he asked

"Sir, please tell me something about bureaucratic system" requested Ram quickly as 'bureaucratic system' word was looking familiar and comfortable to him instead of 'opportunity' theory.

Old man gave a hard look to the novice, thought for a while, drank some water. Obviously he did not like changing gear from opportunity to bureaucracy but somehow ignored and continued

"Mr. Ram, bureaucratic system is like a vehicle, in which boss is like front wheel while subordinates as back wheel.

"And driver?" asked curious Ram

"Bureaucratic system is an automated system – it does not require driver at all. All it needs the efficient synchronization or balancing of front and back wheels"

"Synchronization, balancing, sir I am confused?" asked puzzled Ram

"Look Mr. Ram, bureaucratic system works on coordinated movement of chain of boss-subordinates. For forward movement of the system, subordinates have to follow the boss like -back wheels follow the front wheels. Any lack of synchronization between boss and subordinates is like misalignment of front and back wheel in a vehicle resulting trouble for all"

"What to be done for this synchronization"

"Follow the boss as back wheels follow the front wheels."

"If direction of boss is not right"

"In bureaucratic system one has very limited choice, if boss is not right still one have to follow him like a punctured tyre or unbalanced wheel until one gets some other options. Remember, no one but subordinates loose in case of any failure of synchronization between boss and subordinate" replied exhausted old man.

For good amount of time there was silence in the room. It seems old man was charging his battery while new one was preparing for another question –to clear his confusion or to make himself more confused.

"Sir, here I observed some senior persons and bosses are very good and their subordinates regards them even in their absence ; but cases are also there when some senior persons or bosses not having good reputations among their subordinates and others" asked inquisitive Ram

Old man lit a cigarette, thought for a while before replying

"Mr. Ram in any organization, be it private or government, there are some bosses or managers who are like 'banyan tree', you feel comfort, coolness and protected under them. But at the same time there are many others who are like 'date tree' – they became higher and reach to senior positions over period of time but neither provide any shadow nor fruit to their subordinates or anyone else because they don't have such capability." replied old man

Ram was simply mesmerized with the 'tree theory' of comparison between good and bad managers. Abruptly he asked

"But, sir, how such 'date type' reach so high"

Old man smiled mysteriously and blew the smoke ring.

"Mr. Ram, quite often, particularly in govt. organization, position of a person, is not in accordance of his / her competency but on available vacancy. For example If boss is retiring tomorrow then you, being senior most, is bound to replaced him irrespective of your requisite competency or not. Thus this vacancy based position rather than competency based has elevated many donkeys on the position of the horse over period of time. And pity, they start behaving like horse while inside they have the material of donkey or monkey."

Ram said nothing, mesmerized and perplexed he was simply speechless.

Old man seems to be fully charged after finishing cigarette.

“Sir what I do if I get a ‘date tree’ type boss” asked Ram timidly

“Mr. Ram, you can choose your bride but not your boss”. You are lucky if you get ‘banyan tree’ type boss. However, remember such boss expect absolute loyalty and integrity from their subordinate and don’t mind to go to any extend to punish the guilty, and personally, I feel nothing wrong in it.” Old man paused for a while to take sip of tea and then continued, ‘Date type’ or simply called ‘Toxic bosses’ in management jargon are complex to handle as they are control freak, respect demanding, and difficult to tolerate. Yet they have their own advantage also. As they lack self-confidence and conviction and harbour trust deficit on others thus one can make them depended on oneself by doing some planning, hard work and ignoring their eccentricity and winning their trust. However, only problem in working with toxic bosses is that they never own their subordinates thus hardly protect them in case of any crisis. They believe in principle of ‘my finger is more vulnerable and important than your neck’ thus don’t mind to sacrifice subordinate’s neck to avoid injury to their finger.”

Old man paused for few minutes to charge his exhausted batteries, and lit another cigarette after finishing tea.

Ram preferred to remain silent as he got the sufficient indication that old man did not like interruption during his lecture.

"Mr. Ram, as a subordinate, you are bound to get all type of bosses. Thus you have to learn to manage, adjust and align with them for better synchronization and thus success at work place. Remember, one who works with different type of bosses has better cutting edge over those who had work with only one or two type of bosses. Thus don't afraid of working with any type of boss. After all boss is also human being and thus like any other human being have strength and weakness. Thrive on his strength and encash the weakness to grow."

Ram was not sure whether old man had completed yet or not. He wanted to ask more things but was short of words or knowledge. After long wait he thought it wise to ask interrupted question on opportunity

"Sir, what should be done for creating and encashing the opportunities in bureaucratic system?"

"Creating and en-cashing the opportunities always a long term planning and needs good reputation and understanding not only with immediate boss but also at higher level. However it is too early for you to know such things.

First you learn to develop expertise in making synchronization with all types of bosses as well as your juniors" said old man, looking towards roof and continued after some pause, "Mr. Ram, my last advice to you, if you want to remain satisfy in job as well as in life also- learn to value yourself and your job without caring approval of others."

"Yes sir" replied Ram

There was silence in the room. Old one was tired, exhausted but filled with a sense of satisfaction of educating; young one was overwhelmed and confused yet filled with gratitude.

ABOUT MEETINGS

Today was the last day of Ram's familiarization programme and he was supposed to report to Mr. Banerjee. But there was no one in the office -room. Ram went outside to confirm whether he was in the right room or not. Name was right – R. K. Banerjee, on the name plate.

It was already 11.30 am but office-room was still waiting for its authorized occupant. However presence of spectacle on table and a briefcase on side table was conforming that Mr. Banerjee was not on leave. Nothing to do and nowhere to go, Ram decided to wait for Banerjee in the room itself. He sat down on one of the chair kept opposite to table. Office of Mr. Banerjee was comparatively bigger and better than others and giving enough indications that its occupant was quite methodical. Ram brought out a small note- pad from his newly purchased bag and wondered what lesson he would learn today. As a matter of fact, during past days he had listened too much but understood very less and learned almost nothing. He was feeling lost in the labyrinths of dos and don'ts of bureaucracy. He was having nagging fear about coming days when some work might be given to him. He wondered what he would do as he had forgotten many things about his subjects and 'lessons' of last days. Suddenly he realized that no one had asked him about his subject-knowledge so far. He wondered whether his qualification and subject knowledge would have anything to do with his job in coming time. Looking back to sermons of previous days, it seemed managing boss and getting best out of him or system was bigger concern over here than any other things.

Ram's stream of thought was interrupted with the entry of owner of the room with a diary in his hand and tension on his face. Ram stood up immediately and said good morning. With question mark in his eyes Mr. Banerjee sat on his chair and drank one glass of water from side table. After that he rang up to 2-3 persons, giving them some sort of instructions with politeness mixed authoritative tone.

Mr. Banerjee, in spite of being of 50 plus, had very charming personality.

"Yes, gentleman?" questioned Banerjee with disarming smile and energetic voice.

"Sir, myself Ram, B. Ram exactly, I am new appointee here and supposed to report you today, as part of my familiarization programme" replied Ram quickly

"Yes, I remember" said Mr. Banerjee, bringing out one paper from bottom of one tray and continued, "I was busy in some meeting".

"Yes sir" said Ram

"So what can I do for you gentleman? What type of familiarization do you expect from me?"

Ram thought for few moments and then spoke "Sir, I will be obliged if you tell me something about meeting. What is the purpose of meeting and how it is conducted? Moreover I heard that meeting almost never solve anything and never end on time."

Mr. Banerjee gave a sarcastic look and smile to novice and said "Now, you have joined here so with time you will learn everything including about meetings."

"Sir, you are right but I want to be benefited from your knowledge and experience so that I can learn the things fast."

"Mr. Ram, there are certain things that can't be understood or learnt simply by lecturing. You have to go through the trauma of experiencing them before learning them" replied Banerjee in his usual style of philosophy.

Mr. Banerjee, though at senior position yet very simple, knowledgeable and was easily approachable. His human quotient was much higher than bureaucratic one. Earlier he was a lecturer in an academic institution but charm of better remuneration dragged him into marshy land of bureaucracy.

"Sir, you are right, even than I want to listen and learn from your experience and knowledge" persisted Ram.

Mr. Banerjee did not reply but lit a cigarette from freshly opened packet. He always enjoyed meeting with young persons – energetic and non-polluted; it enlivened innate teacher in him. After a long pause, with cigarette in one hand and thick spectacles in other, he said

"Mr. Ram, meetings are necessary evil of bureaucracy"

"Then why meetings are conducted" asked impatient Ram

"Meeting are conducted to serve broadly following purpose" replied Banerjee, having experience of 20 years in attending meetings of various types.

'To convey the message that you are being monitored'

'To remind you about authority of boss'

'To form a committee to avoid a decision or responsibility on contentious issues'

Ram quickly took mental note of above. His mental faculty was at maximum alert as he did not want to lose any word of Mr. Banerjee's sermon.

Mr. Banerjee paused for some time then continued "Meetings are usually of following types"

- Information getting meetings
- Authoritative meetings
- Decision making meetings
- Time pass meetings

Information Getting Meeting

"Such meetings are shortest way to get distorted and half-baked information about anything in the world through some presentation given by some highly courteous representative of some company, desperately looking for business for its outdated models or obsolete technology on the cost of ignorance of attendees.

Many times 'informative' presentations are also given by some in house 'experts', who know the price of everything but value of nothing, The sole motto of these 'importance hungry' experts is to impress all those who matters by doing 'something' on the cost of the Company that help in boosting their importance and career rather than bottom line of the Company.

In such meetings there are always some 'born enlighten' and 'Iknow all' types experts. Nothing can hold these 'experts' from speaking in such meetings. The only problem with them is that they don't when to speak and whether participants are interested to listen them or not. Fortunately, there are good 'born contradictor' who reins these born-experts. These 'experts and contradictors' enlivens such otherwise boring meeting and also help in keeping all passive listeners awaken.

This type of meeting is not to take any decision but to 'educate' bosses and their sycophants (chamcha) about anything in the world and invariably end up without leaning of anything of worth or any decision of importance."

AUTHORITATIVE MEETING

"This type of meeting is called to remind subordinates about boss authority. There is no apparent agenda of such meeting except to rebuke some targeted one on some flimsy ground to give the message to others that they must not undermine the authority of the boss.

"But, sir, how someone can be rebuked without any reasons and that too in the presence of others" interrupted the puzzled Ram

Banerjee gave a smile and continued, "Mr. Ram, in any organization there are three types of subordinates.

- One who can bow down to some extend.
- Secondly -who can bow down to any extend
- Third type is hard to make bow down or simply they are defiant type.

A successful boss knows very well whom to be rebuked or not. Boss prefer to rebuke second category i.e. easy to bow down type subordinates, as they can't dare to be defiant. Such subordinates are the favourite target of boss to show the authority to others. For such subordinates boss is like God and they forget boss's rebuking very easily and indulge again in pleasing their master i. e boss and eventfully able to win his favors also.

Usually good boss avoid taking head -on third category especially in this type of meeting. However the boss remains in search of all possible opportunities to tighten the screws of such defiant ones subordinates.

Decision taking meeting

"This type of meeting is not common and held only when things reach to dead end or buck can't be passed any further on the pretext of matter refer to this or that or committee has been formed or simply when further delay can't be afforded etc.

Decision, being a single point responsibility, always put its taker in tight corner thus all members of meeting prefer to or pretend to be tense in tacit support of the boss during this sort of meeting"

Time pass Meeting

"This type of meetings are necessary evil of any organization particularly of govt. Whether you like it or not, you have to give company to boss, either in meeting or any other occasions, to help him pass time as a official decorum or to show your allegiance to him.".

"Usually these type of meetings are held at the fag -end of day." said Banerjee in the tone of a lecturer and continued after taking water "In such meeting number of persons present are more than agenda points to be discussed. Such time pass meetings are the best place for many ones to keep them busy and remain important without doing work of any worth. Cycle purchasing meeting, cycle distribution meeting, anomaly in cycle distribution meeting, Cycle maintenance contract meeting, cycle theft , cycle write off, fortnightly Hindi meeting, arbitration meeting, safety meeting etc and etc are the offshoots of time pass meeting. Attending seminar, presentations, workshop etc are value added products of time pass meetings" said the enlighten ones who had lost half of his hair in attending meeting but not the zeal to learn the new things, new lesson.

"Sir, I am confused up to my toes and don't know what I do when I will be given responsibilities to attend the meetings" pleaded novice one

Enlightened one thought for a moment, saw directly in the eyes of Ram and said "Mr. Ram, if you remember the following rules, you will become expert in short time in giving reply in meetings."

- Avoid arguments in meetings. Don't defend your point too much. Listen carefully, answer respectfully and always say less than necessary. Open your card wisely. Let some guess work to be done by others.

- Master the art of passing the bucks to others politely. If you do the things right it is fine. If not, then you must know how to answer the things in meetings without hurting self and offending others and how to pass the bucks to others.

- Develop expertise in shifting the spot light or focus of meeting to others

- Never say empathic 'NO' as well as 'YES'. In other word don't commit any thing in meeting. If required simply say "I will look into it, sir".

"Mr. Ram, meetings and tea –these two are indispensable part of any company. You have choice about tea but not for meeting. And when you don't have any choice, you have to develop expertise to survive 'honorably'. If you follow even 50% of what you have been told, you will learn to survive honorably in the maze of bureaucracy. You are new and have a long way to go thus -one last piece of advice. Always keep alive the desire to learn new things, new lessons. This will help you enliven your life among dead things of bureaucracy.

There was silence in the room. Ram was not able to find appropriate words to show his gratitude to Banerjee sir. Suddenly ringing of telephone broke the silence and gave the message that that another meeting will be held after one hour. Banerjee body language gave the indication that he want to be left alone. Ram thought it prudent to leave the room.

Ram wrote following in his diary

My familiarization part is now over. I don't know what to write about my this part. I have mixed feeling. During these I met so many persons some are very good and knowledgeable while others are ok – like everywhere, like my college days. This world is mixed of good or bad. There is nothing absolute good or bad in this world. I don't know what role I have to play here, in the Company. I wish to contribute with best of my ability and capability for the progress of the Company. I read somewhere that *A Company progress for its employees and with its employees.* But like everywhere, here also some employees are very good while some are---

I still remembered what Old man told me other day

In upper management some managers are like banyan tree, you feel comfort and coolness and feel protected under them . But there are many who are like date tree – they became higher but neither provide any shadow nor fruit.

And one must learn to adjust with both type

PART II

PROFESSIONAL

With passing of time they had become real "professional". In meetings they quarreled, they shout and never let go smallest opportunities to pull legs of others like "enemies" but next morning they become "friends" as nothing happened on previous day. After all, this all was in the interest of work.

With time they had transformed to seasoned professional and hard core opportunist from simple human beings. They didn't mind to sacrifice 'friendship' and never missed any opportunity to cut down the size of others for gaining slightest benefit in their favor. More higher they moved, more seasoned professional they became. For them, management means ensuring their healthy survival and for it always ready to 'cut' the throat of others in anticipation of danger on their finger. After all, my penny had more worth than diamond of yours.

Mr. Jani also belonged to such professional species. Smiling face and soft spoken. Hard to believe that beneath this smiling face lies a hard core opportunist and cold blood professional

A dangerous mind behind the veil of innocuous face.

Mr. Jani, I/c safety, used to make routine visit to his area before going to meeting. He firmly believed in seeing the things with his own eyes rather than listening them from subordinates. Probably due to the fact that 'hidden opportunity' could be best understood by seeing rather than hearing. Things that eyes can perceive, ear can't. This habit had helped him in reaping 'rich dividend' on many occasions.

But purpose of today visit was somewhat different. He was reported by one junior that one light fitting was lying in broken condition in his area, fallen probably due to heavy wind in night.

"Where is the light fitting" MrJani inquired

"Sir at that side" replied the junior officer and escorted him, with alertness and enthusiasm, at the spot where broken light fitting was lying.

Mr. Jani inspected the broken light fitting from every angle as experienced policeman see the body of a dead victim. After some thinking, Mr. Jani raised his head to look the place where unfortunate light once used to hang with pride. Junior officer could not understand what point Jani sir, was looking for. For him it was not such an important thing that needs so much concentration from such a senior officer. A light fitting had fallen from height due to heavy wind, thus no one could be blamed for it, and to avoid recurrence of such incidence all hanging light -fittings needed to be check for tightness. However what he could not understand the hidden opportunity in this fallen light. The hidden opportunity that need clever mind of Mr. Jani to understand, to en -cash and also to settle the score with Mr. Ganeshan, I/c maintenance, who had not "helped" him on many occasions and particularly in getting repaired of refrigerator at his home.

"Sir, I want to draw the attention of the august house on near miss major accident on previous night that could have taken precious life of one of our employee. Luckily he escaped narrowly, fortunate for him and his family and as well as for all of us"; Jani continued with best of his rhetoric; "as all of you know that how stringent are laws of Labor Commissioner on the issue of safety of personnel. As a safety officer, I am very much concerned about the state of affair of maintenance of electrical items".

There was pin drop silence in meeting for a moment. Rhetoric of safety officer, Mr. Jani, had worked as all eyes moved towards Mr. Ganeshan, in charge of maintenance, the culprit in witness box.

Mr. Ganeshan, a perfect gentleman with not so perfect rhetoric. He could face technical problems bravely but not the people. A simple and straightforward man in not so straightforward world.

"Sir one light had fallen in night and incident took place due to heavy wind in night sir" Ganeshan spoke in shaky voice

"Don't say it is an incident, it is an accident" shouted Jani. "There is no maintenance, light fitting has rusted badly and falling from height like mango from tree in wind"

A little laughter lightens the atmosphere but not the situation.

"Sir, we have already started tightening all light fitting and taking all possible measures to avoid reoccurrence of such happening" said Ganeshan, looking towards boss for rescue.

Boss was having soft corner for Ganeshan, partly for his sincerity, but mainly for the reason that both Ganeshan and he hailed from same geographical area. But time was not right for showing the affection in the presence of all.

"Mr. Ganeshan, this should not happened in future and find out the reason why light has fallen like this" boss said in coarse voice, trying to be as hard as possible.

"Sir, seeing the seriousness of the matter and condition of the fallen light- fitting, a committee should be formed to find out the reason to avoid recurrence of such incident in future" proposed by Mr. Jani and instantly supported by some others members who believed forming an committee is ultimate solution of all problems of the world.

Thus a committee was formed, comprising In –charge Maintenance, In – charge Procurement and, of course, In –charge Safety to give their recommendation within 30 days.

Except I/c charge Maintenance, Mr. Ganeshan, committee was of the opinion that all light fitting should be change. After initial protest Ganeshan also gave up and signed the recommendation of committee to replace all lights fittings.

I/c Procurement was happy a lot. After all, a new good order will come up shortly.

I/c Safety was happy. After all, his brother – in- law, supplier of electrical things will also get a chance and if things fall in line, may get the order also.

I/c Maintenance was happy. After all new lights won't require any maintenance for pretty long time.

LOGIC

"Sir, it is not logical to execute this job" said new young subordinate enthusiastically as if he had discovered 'Eureka'

Boss gave him a hard look and replied, "I told you to prepare the estimate for the job not to find the logic"

"But sir, I can prove executing this work will be a wasteful expenditure and not add--.

"You are working in a Govt. Company; you need not to worry about economics of things but carrying out the order. Moreover, order for doing this work is received from Head Quarter thus you need not to prove anything but to execute it without any second thought ". Boss interrupted him in between

"But sir, you should apprise big bosses at H.Q. and tell them executing this job is not logical and will add to wasteful expenditure" continued subordinate stubbornly.

"H.Q. orders are for compliance and not for arguments or to protest" replied boss feebly.

As a matter of fact, boss also had the feeling that this order was not right and would only add to wasteful expenditure but experience of last 20 years had made him seasoned enough to overlook the logics and simply comply the orders. He knew very well the fate and cost of protesting such orders. But this new subordinate--, if not controlled, would land him also in trouble.

"But sir, doing something without logic is-----" persisted the subordinate

"Come to office without wearing your logic, simply shoes and clothes are sufficient" replied boss firmly

"But sir, I am not feeling comfortable doing it" said the subordinate defiantly

"As long as one gets pay and promotion in time he or she must not feel uncomfortable"

"But sir -----

"Nothing doing, either do the job as you have been told or give in writing that you can't do it" boss gave him the final verdict.

Subdued subordinate remained silent in distress and eventually stands up to leave. Boss looked towards him. In fact he did not want to be so harsh. After all, this boy had untainted intention. He thought for a moment then beckoned him to sit down and said

"Look, I did not mean to hurt you but we all are working in a system where we get our pay to comply the order of our seniors, not to judge right or wrong in it. This is hard fact but it is required to run the system. And system is – subordinates have to comply the order of seniors without questioning or analyzing right or wrong in it. May be bosses or seniors sitting at HQ having wider vision or compulsion that probably we may not be able to understand. Thus you simply execute the job as per order and don't waste your time and energy in thinking of economy and similar sort of things otherwise you will be dumped in waste basket."

Subordinate looked blankly on one of the poster hanging on the wall, behind boss's chair 'Dedication, Transparency and Productivity – Company policy' written in capital letters along with some obscure picture. Suddenly he asked "Sir, what will happen when production will not increase even after spending so much money".

"Our job is to execute the things not to see its objectives and expenditure. Moreover, by the time this job will get completed, most of the persons associated with it will be transferred to other places.

Even if not transferred, there are thousands of ways of justifying the things from both ends, if things go wrong. So gentleman, take my advice, forget worrying about 'future things' and think about clearing 'present thing or danger' to remain safe and in good book of your seniors. Thus, go ahead as per order and clear present things" advised boss.

Subordinate weighed his choices logically and concluded that virtually he had only one choice. He had to clear the present things to earn his pay 'honorably'.

COLLECTIVE MISTAKE

"Sir, there is a serious mistake in file thus making whole thing wrong" said enthusiastic subordinate, pointing towards the mistakes in calculation

"Why have you not pointed it earlier? It had already signed by so many senior officers" inquired worried boss

"Sir I am new here and file is old, before my joining".

Boss did not reply. He was at a loss.

"Should I record this mistake in file and re-work the things?" asked novice

Boss thought for a moment. The file belongs to his office and all other senior officers have signed after his signature. Thus being initiator, it was full responsibility of his section to check everything before sending the file to senior officers. Pointing out basic error after such a long journey of file would not only annoy all seniors but also put question mark over his authenticity and sincerity. He was in a fix. Over and above, it was time of filling

Performance report; pointing out the mistake at this juncture would definitely annoyed seniors and this might jeopardize his performance report and thus promotion. He thought for a moment and then spoke

"No, you need not to record any such thing in file; it is too late now and thus continues the things as it is".

'But sir' subordinate hesitated

"You are new here so do as I am saying for your own benefit otherwise you will suffer for pointing out the mistakes of seniors"

Subdued subordinate did not utter any word but kept looking towards floor. He did not know what to say or do

Seeing his dilemma, boss advised

'Look, many senior officers have already signed in this file thus every signatory has become responsible to some extent so nothing will happen even if something goes wrong. Moreover, in Govt. Company there is no punishment for Collective mistake'.

Subordinate saw towards boss as he found some logic in boss suggestion – no punishment for collective mistakes

'And what should I do with file' asked half-convinced subordinate

'Keep on rolling the file without being rolled down under it by taking more and more signature in it. More signature file has more safe it become' whispered experienced boss

'But sir, how long we can keep on rolling the file'

'Till it reach at dead end or suitable scapegoat is found' said the boss with glittering eyes.

SAFEGUARD

Vendor selection meeting was in progress. After lot of deliberations and discussion for last 2 days, now time had come to short-list the vendor for the job.

"You know, today, we have to final the short-listing of the vendors" said principal member of the committee named Srinivasan.

Mr. Srinivasan, egoistic, hard speaking and un-compromising, enjoying powerful position in bureaucratic pecking order, owing to his seniority rather than capabilities. Heading any committee gave him immense sense of pride.

"But sir, short listed vendors are of poor track records while good and reputed vendors are being rejected" said Mr. Paul, under whose supervision prestigious job was to be executed.

"Mr. Paul, purpose of this committee is to short -list the vendors strictly as per guidelines and evaluation criteria rather than looking into the reputation or track record of the vendors" replied Srinivasan philosophically

"Sir, everyone present here know very well that one of the rejected vendor has excellent track record" persisted worried Paul

"But his papers are not complete" replied one 'passive member' of the committee to show his presence as well as support to powerful Srinivasan

"But this vendor is meeting all important and vital criteria of evaluations and also leader in type of work to be executed here" continued Paul, whose only concern was to get the good vendors for this important work.

"Mr. Paul, this vendor of repute, as you are saying, has not signed on page no 249 of bidding documents and also not submitted papers in accordance of rules stipulated on page no 25 "replied Srinivasan and continued sarcastically "I don't know how a bidder so casual in papers can be good in doing work"

"Rejecting some good vendor just because one signature or one silly paper out of thousand is missing while fulfilling all vital criteria, is not justifiable" defended Paul and continued after some pause" moreover, sir, it is not proper to stick on some small "should things" while all "must things" have been complied by the vendor"

"Don't be emotional, Mr. Paul, office is not run on emotion but on rules, regulations and guidelines. And as per guidelines the vendor is not fulfilling all the requirement, whatsoever it may be, big or small, thus has to be rejected" said Srinivasan firmly.

"Sir, we can ask clarification from bidder," asked one 'sleeping' member of the committee, awaken by pleading of Mr. Paul and harsh voice of Mr. Srinivasan

"Better you update yourself before giving suggestion", replied Mr. Srinivasan acidly and continued, "as per new Head Quarter guidelines, no clarification can be asked from any vendor once bids are opened "

Awaken member again entered into his shell after being rebuked. There was silence in the room. After all, who can dare to go against Srinivasan? Powerful, knowledgeable (or well informed) and filled to the brim with ego.

Mr. Paul, work –oriented with all honest intentions, was a worried lot.

The job was important and a bad vendor would mess all the things and make his life hell. But he was helpless, as he did not have the authority to select the vendor and people who have the authority are more concerned about written-things but least bothered about 'facts –things'. They keep their eyes wide open but mind shut and locked. They were doing the job of clerk on the salary and post of managers. Their job was to separate straw from wheat but---

They were safeguarding themselves to the extent of wearing helmet in the car.

"Sir, should we ask the clarification from HQ on this issue?" asked Paul suddenly, with the glimmer in his eyes as if found some ray of hope in dark tunnel of pessimism.

"We are very clear in our mind that we are not going to violate the written things- thus no point of asking clarification" said Srinivasan crisply, glancing over his wrist-watch and then other members of the committee, enough indication for them that no more beating around the bush and decision is final.

Powerful persons don't change their decision for the weak ones. There is no point of arguing with them about right or wrongs of things.

"But, sir don't you feel it is rubbish that we are rejecting such a good vendor on such flimsy ground" said frustrated Paul, trying his best to keep his words and frustration in control.

"Maybe flimsy for you but not for the people who have to put their signatures on papers" said Srinivasan tersely

"But sir, in the interest of the work..,"

Paul futile attempt to influence the lost battle was interrupted in between

"Mr. Paul, we all must be more interested to safeguard our own interest first. And yours, mine and others safeguard lies in following the written things only- without analysis or interpretation" replied Srinivasan in final word and beckoned for finishing of the meeting.

They assembled to:

- disapprove the approved things.
- crucify the crux of things to safeguard themselves not the Company

STETHOSCOPE

"Doctor is good one, has excellent track record and meeting our requirement" exclaimed Mr. Sufferer with a sigh of relief.

"But doctor's stethoscope is not matching with our specifications" uttered Mr. Cautious, busy in browsing and shuffling some papers.

Mr. Experience looked towards Mr. Cautious and said "In that case we can't appoint the doctor."

"But sir, doctor has excellent record" protested Mr. Sufferer

"So what? We have to go by guide lines and what is written in the rules -book and. It is clearly mentioned on page no 52 that doctor and stethoscope both should match our specification for acceptance" replied Mr. Cautious empathically.

"But sir, rejecting a good doctor because of something in stethoscope is not justifiable".

"What is written in the rule- book has to be followed word by word" added Mr. Experience and continued "You are new here that is why don't understand the complication of such things".

"But sir, we must not read the rules with closed mind" persisted Mr. Sufferer

"We can't closed our career by opening our mind" reacted Mr. Cautious sharply and continued "Mr. Sufferer you don't know how difficult are things in today atmosphere because of Mr. Suspicious. The only way to remain protected from powerful Mr. Suspicious is to follow what is written in rules-book religiously word by word without any thinking and logics".

Mr. Experience nodded with agreement and added further fuel "you are new here thus don't understand the implications of such things. Had you been aware of the case of Mr. Enthusiastic, you would have different approach. Mr. Enthusiastic promotion is pending since last 3 years even though his work was widely appreciated by top management."

"Why sir?asked Mr. Sufferer curiously"

"Because he had violated the holy rule- book as per Mr. Suspicious 'doubt' report"

"But Mr. Enthusiastic is very honest I know him personally" said Mr. Sufferer with disbelief and surprise in his eyes.

"The only yardstick of the honesty is how religiously one follows the rule- book and maintained the status quo" suggested Mr. Experience and continued "In zeal of doing things quickly and timely, Mr. Enthusiasm landed himself in the circle of uncertainty. He succeeded in work but failed in managing his career as he caught the attention of Mr. Suspicious for bypassing the system and breaking the status quo."

Accused of violating the status quo, not for dishonesty.

Accused of doing right things in wrong ways, not for doing wrong for money.So what if doing so helped in averting huge loss to the company.

Mr. Sufferer was feeling dejected. Still he was not convinced why a good doctor was being rejected. He thought about all the efforts he had done in reaching up to this stage. He thought about all the good time he devoted to expedite the things – but all in vain just because of something written somewhere was meant to be followed blindly without logics and question to remain safe. Or otherwise should be ready to pay the price of violating status quo like Mr. Enthusiasm- succeeded in work but failed in managing career. He looked toward Mr. Cautious and Mr. Experience, doing post-mortem of another case unperturbedly, probably looking for 'dead doctor' having 'live stethoscope'.

PROMOTION

Boss - "Congratulation, Mr. X, you have been promoted. This time you are lucky."

X- "No need of congratulation sir, I don't want any promotion now"

Boss: What! Why?

X- "Because I am happy with my present position. I have already given in writing that I don't want any promotion"

Boss- "Have you become mad"? "OK. I understand you deserve it long back but it is always better to be late than never".

X- "It is better not to get the things if you don't get them in time".

Boss- "Do you feel promotion is your right?

X- "No sir, it is the right of those who do everything but not the work"

Boss remained silent, thinking for the better words to convince X

X also remained silent with forlorn look on his face. After completing his degree from top institute, he joined this Company, with enthusiasm and big hope. But now after 20 years, he was disillusioned.

In spite of working very hard years together in the harsh field condition he did not get the promotion. But what truly pained him was the way others proven inefficient, posted at soft place, were promoted. Not only his colleague even juniors and lesser qualified, loyal to their bosses rather than Company, were also rewarded.

Year after year, once the list is out, he begin to receive endless sympathy. He gets to know from so many corners that he is so worthy. Everybody tells him that how much deserving he is and how big an injustice that the system has been doing by not promoting him. And now he decided not to endure further promotion related pain.

Boss- "Mr. X, I advice you not to play with your career. You still have long innings"

X- "Sir, I stop thinking about my career years back when I did not get the promotion and my juniors and lesser qualified persons got it because of the reasons you or management may be knowing better. For me now, there are plenty more important things in life than my career".

Boss didn't speak anything. He knew it well that injustice was done with X. Even though he was hard working and brilliant yet had been left out far behind in the rat race of promotion due to his 'work oriented rather than boss oriented attitude'. He still remembered the day when he tried to convince big- boss about X.

"How a person having such defiant attitude can be promoted. Such person becomes pain in ass if given promotion. Only 'obedient ones' can be elevated to higher post." replied big- boss.

"But sir, X has excellent record as far as work is concern" he defended .

"For that he is getting pay" big-boss told indifferently and gave the indication that he didn't want further discussion on this topic.

There was quietness in the room. X was quiet, looking outside of the window's glass from boss's room, but boss was perturbed. Somehow he had the feeling of burden on his conscience of not defending X promotion case vigorously. Probably due to fear of displeasing the big-boss.

Boss- "Look Mr. X, I am your well wisher, you got the promotion and you must join it. I will see it should not happen in future"

X- "But sir, I don't deserve promotion this time because I had not contributed anything of worth to the Company during last 2 years"

Boss -"It must be due to your past achievement"

X- "Then sir, promotion must be from back date but it is not."

Boss- "Mr. X, will you achieve anything by this stand?"

X- "Of course, personally I will be looser but I will be gainer if my stand forces the Management to review the 'Frustration policy' on the name of promotion policy. It looks promotion is being given not because of one's ability and hard work but of generosity of boss. That is promoting culture of sycophancy as everyone is more concerned for boss generosity rather than welfare of the Company, giver of our bread & butter."

Boss- "Do you feel that you alone can change the system?".

X- "I don't know. All I know is that accepting this promotion will not give solace to my mental agony".

Boss- "Do you feel you are the alone who are the victim of this promotion policy? There are so many including myself who have been victimized. But what can we do. We are the part of the system and have to live with it. We can't go against of it whether get promotion or not. We have to be practical."

X- "Thank you for your practical advises, sir. But everyone cannot be as practical as you are. Someone has to say "NO" to injustice or wrong things if we feel this is our company. Someone has to give answer what for person like me being punished – for not doing the work efficiently or not doing the sycophancy (efficiently). I have always respected my seniors but I can't stoop to please them. This is a govt. company and every employee own it but few powerful have made it their personal play ground with the team of sycophants".

There was long drawn silence in the room. Boss knew X was right

Suddenly, X stand up and left the room.

Boss also left the room to apprise big- boss about defiant attitude of Mr. X

Not getting promotion- think again

More promotion you get more freedom you lose to say NO.

In management practices, many a times, The Peter principle and the Dilbert principle are applied while considering employees for promotions. The principles are

Peter Principle holds that 'Competent people are routinely promoted until they reach a level of incompetence'.

The Dilbert Principle suggests that 'Incompetent employees are often promoted to management positions simply to prevent further damage in working ranks'.

Scott Adam (creator of Dilbert Principle) said Dilbert principle succeeded the Peter Principle that 'Every employee is promoted to one level above to his state of competence.

STIFLING EFFICIENY

There was a lot of flutter in the office.

Reason?

Mr. Narayan, the most promising, intelligent, dynamic, smiling and always doing some work or busy in discussing some problem has submitted his resignation. Mr. Narayan, a supportive colleague, an outstanding dependable subordinate and an excellent senior to a few lucky juniors. In short he was a complete package of good human being and excellent professional.

Resigning a govt. job and promising future in the world of uncertainty was bound to create some flutter.

"Why has he resigned? Has he gone insane?" asked someone

"May be some private company has offered him big jump. Probably he might be offered one or two promotion by some outside company. After all, he is so outstanding." answered some other.

"But he is not money minded I am sure, I know him for many years. Money is not his priority, for him money is simply a tool not an objective of life." defended one friend

"Then why he had resigned?" inquired one inquisitive mind

None but Narayan could answer it best.

And Narayan was sitting in front of committee, given the job to find out the reason of his resignation from the Company, offering one of the best pay packages. And also suggest the remedies to stop such resignation.

"So Mr. Narayan, you have decided to resign" asked senior most member of the committee

Narayan nodded but said nothing.

"We hope you will tell us frankly reason of your resignation" continued senior member

"Sir, I believe you will also analyze the reasons of my resignation with open mind as my feeling is not of mine only but of many" answer confident Narayan

"Mr. Narayan, you know our Company offer one of the best pay package in the industry and also one of the best employer thus you have great future ahead in the Company" said another member of the committee

"Yes sir, I know"

"Then what is the reason of your resignation?" inquired another member

"Sir, I feel that I am not able to deliver my best here."

"Why"?

"Sir, I wanted to do many big things for the Company but I was not allowed to. I feel my hands are tied and wings are clipped here due to unnecessary rules & regulations. I am not alone, there are many among file and ranks of the Company who harbor this feeling of stifling but they may have their own reason to bear all this but I can't take it anymore. That is why I have decided to quit before I become used to of this stifling and become rusted. I can't bear the fact anymore that finalization of simple, small things not only takes months but sometimes years together due to absurd rules and regulations and inefficiency of system. A lot of information, lengthy discussion but few decision and still fewer implementation and even fewer success. No one wants to take any corrective action or tweaking the rules as everyone prefers to work in safe mode out of fear. In today competitive environment when time is everything and timely decision makes all the difference such delay and indecision are beyond my tolerance any more. I tried to adjust myself like others but I feel frustrated and stifled now."

Committee members became stunned with this outburst of Mr. Narayan. Suddenly they felt themselves on receiving end and in defensive mode.

"Mr. Narayan ours is the govt. company thus we have to follow certain govt. directive on many issues irrespective of agreeing or not. Thus ours hand are also tied on some issues as we are answerable to govt." replied senior member of the committee in defense

"Sir I understand your limitation. I agree removal of hurdles is not in your hand but lowering the height of these hurdles, easing these hurdles and tweaking of unnecessary rules are definitely in the hands of powerful persons like you. But sadly no attempt is being made for the same. Everyone is interested to maintain the status quo in fear of action. No one wants to bell the cat. Everyone is in illusion that nothing will happen to the Company. The Company is suffering not because of inefficiency and inaction of its people but because of inefficiency of the system. People are talented and interested to do the work but system is not allowing them by one way or others. Their efficiencies are stifling and talents are rusting. Sir, do something before it become too late. Administer the medicine before patient die.

There was silence among committee members as they knew M. Narayan was right.

Mr. Narayan left the room and the company as well.

One more who dared to flew in open sky rather than keep on ruing for clipped wings.

One more whose feeling of stifling became more severe than comfort of status quo and assurance of next month pay

One more who decided not to be get rusted anymore in constrained atmosphere of do and don't.

Committee submitted his censored report. One more report to give company to dusting gathering reports. Business was as usual. Probably, somewhere another Narayan was struggling to cope up with his stifling in hope of some action, some improvement.

URGENT MEETING

Urgent meeting was going on. Fear mixed sincerity and seriousness was written on the face of everyone.

Agenda: Visit of new Chairman, known for his no nonsense and intolerance.

"Where are the agenda points of last visit of Chairman?" asked worried boss, transferred here few months back from other place.

"Sir, earlier Chairman came here only once and that too at the time of retirement for farewell so those agenda points will not be valid for new Chairman. We have to frame new agenda based" said Pandeyji, sitting next to boss.

New boss didn't like Pandeyji but at this time of need he had no choice but to listen him as he was most experience in the house. Moreover he had made all arrangement during visit of earlier Chairman.

However, Pandeyji, master manipulator, with link at H.Q., was also worried this time. New Chairman had come from other company. Report about him was very disturbing. He had already suspended two persons on the charge of dereliction of duty and had shifted many "indispensable pillars" to dump yard. This new Chairman had shaken the 'established system'.

"This new Chairman doesn't understand the culture of our company thus won't survive" expert foretold emphatically. But he survived and had made survival of the 'well-wishers' of the Company difficult.

And now, on Monday, this 'alien - predator' was schedule to visit here, much to fear and discomfort of many. Fear, anxiety and seriousness was written on the face of all 'powerful' who were supposed to attend meeting with new Chairman. And in their anxiety, they had made the life of their subordinates more difficult by asking all sorts of data, reports, presentations etc from them. After all, no one knew what this new Chairman would say or ask.

More powerful are you, more worried you have to be.

Boss was worried a lot. He was due for promotion and if his impression during Chairman visit was not good then----. Or, worst he might also be shifted (dumped) to some corner like one of his colleague. He hurriedly wiped his face with crumbled handkerchief. However there was one silver lining, he and this new chairman were of same caste. But will this mad Chairman consider it? "I have to work out some strategy to tell him that I belong to him" He whispered to self and tried to concentrate in meeting.

Most experienced, master manipulator, Pandeyji was also worried. He was at this seat of power since so many years and till now had succeeded in manipulating his transfer due to his link in H.Q. But this new Chairman – he had already transferred so many indispensable and powerful from green-pasture to remote and dry places. "Somehow I have to manage to remain here. I have left 3 years in my retirement and transfer at this stage ---. I have to do something" whispered Pandeyji to self and tried to concentrate in the meeting.

Mr. Sinha, was worried up to his toes. There was strong rumour that some of his files were being investigated by vigilance. Mr. Sinha was a 'protected species' in the regime of old Chairman thus no one dared to touch him so far. But after coming of new Chairman 'protected species became 'endangered species'.

All this started from his daughter recent lavish marriage, attended by who is who of the company. The highly lavish marriage created the ripples and some ripples reached to new Chairman. Soon ripples converted into tide, having enough force to change lion of protected species into a lamb. First time in his long 'illustrious' career Sinhaji was feeling insecure and helpless. All of his well wishers, friends and even beneficiaries started deserting him. No one wanted to be shown as closed to him. It is real "Kal- Yug", Sinhaji whispered to self in distress and tried to concentrate in meeting but in vain.

Others were also worried, albeit not as much as mighty ones. However reasons of their worry were different – 'What would happen to them if mighty ones transferred or worst suspended?' After all, their well being was also directly proportional to well beings of their bosses.

Urgent meeting was going on in an atmosphere of fear, anxiety and uncertainty to frame the agenda so that best can be shown on the carpet while sweeping all dust under carpet.

LAMB v/s LION

Mr. Anand, section boss, was upset.

Big boss had pulled him in meeting on small matter. Mr. Anand never spoke anything in his defence or even react to big boss no matter how much he was banged or rebuked for reason or without reason. Mr. Anand belonged to that tribe of subordinates who can absorb any amount of firing from higher up but hardly react. For them boss is like God thus they forget boss's rebuking easily and quickly and again indulged in pleasing their master to win his favours.

However, surprisingly, they have entirely different attitude once they come in their territory, as a boss.

Thus, on reaching his room, Mr. Anand called the meeting of the subordinates working under him to vent out his anger. His worries was not to dig out the real problem and improve but to pass on his anger to subordinates' officers, to remind them his authority

A lamb became lion.

Defender became attacker.

Subordinate became boss

Tail of tiger became head of lambs.

Mr. Anand had the reputation of rough talking (to his subordinates obviously). He was firm believer of the policy that subordinates have to be kept terrorized to extract best from them while boss must be polished to take best from him. He always remained in search of opportunists to pull and rebuked his subordinates.

So today meeting was to percolate the message that if I was banged I would bang all of you.

Meeting started. Mr. Boss was red-faced.

Everyone was surprised by this unscheduled meeting. Everyone was apprehensive and defensive.

Mr. boss stared everyone present in the meeting

Like inspector stared to culprits.

Like lion stares helpless lamb.

"You know today I was forced to listen unpleasant words from big- boss just because of inefficiency and carelessness of you people".

"I tell you that I won't listen anything on account of you", Mr. boss continued Everyone was silent, silent not because of fear but because of system, system of boss-subordinates relation, system of office decorum, system in which a donkey can rule over horses. A system that makes a lamb to lion.

TIME TO CAPITALISE

It was time of change

Mr. Old was about to shown door, albeit honorably (retiring). Mr. New was about to welcome in enthusiastically.

Dusk was reluctant to go into darkness but Dawn was eager to turn into brightness.

It was the time of change; It was the time of lot of activities.

Time to bid adieu to Mr. Old and praise him, tell him how good he was, even if he was not

Time to welcome Mr. New and show him how good are we.

Opportunists were busy in extracting maximum from Mr. Old before dumping him.

Sycophants were busy in showing their loyalty to Mr. New

Farewell committee was being formed-volunteers were hard to find.

Welcome committee was also being formed -volunteers were stumbling upon one another to come in.

Some omnipresent wanted to be in both the committee; for them being in limelight is important than events.

Farewell committee was searching suitable gift for outgoing as last ritual of burial of his memories

Welcome committee was busy in knowing the liking / disliking of incoming and showing him best of ours

Mr. In – new father of the family, earning head, very important and very useful.

Mr. Out – now grandfather of family, important but not useful-like heritage building.

Of course, Mr. Old was good but now has dead future; Mr. New may not be as good but has live future.

Future alive v/s Future dead

Rising Sun v/s setting Sun

Both have its importance but only rising Sun have future, worth and usefulness thus worshipped

And opportunists and sycophants worshipped nothing but 'usefulness' only.

LOVE SAFETY

Safety week observance was in progress like last year or before that. Everyone had clear instructions that they have to wear the helmet as a senior person would visit at work area any time. Suddenly there was scramble for helmets. All of sudden helmet became important and over to head.

Upon much request, store keeper also arranged 'lost' helmets from other places – after all today it was the matter of safety.

And when senior officer visited along with safety officer everyone was wearing the helmet. It looked 'helmet on head' was a way to salute the senior officers, to give regards to them -for visiting their work area. So everyone was wearing helmet except senior officer and safety officer. After all, they were seniors and have to be identified separately. Moreover being Senior they were safety proof nothing can happens to them.

"This year safety slogan is "Love Safety; Live Safely" announced Safety officer. And distributed safety award to some chosen one for last year 'performance'

"We all should take the oath to make this year an accident free year" senior officer preached before leaving.

Moments after departure of senior officer and safety officer,proud helmets were removed from head to get fresh air on head and mind. Store keeper collected them to put them safely.

I/C of the work was worried about meeting the work - target while meeting all safety norms and slogan of Love safety; Live safely.

Job evaders were happy for having one more excuse of avoiding the work in the disguise of safety norms. For them slogan was Love safety; Hate the job.

SUGGESTION

Review meeting was in progress. Everyone was in attentive mode, browsing minutes of previous meeting and mentally preparing the reply to be given.

"Mishraji, why this job could not be finalized so far? There is no progress since last meeting. What is happening here?" inquired big-boss with dismay

Mishraji, a fat belly person, known for his outright views and straightforwardness, remained silent for few seconds as he was not sure what to reply.

Roaming eyes of big -boss again focused on Mishraji in expectation of answer.

"Sir, during, last 15 days there were many meetings like, cycle purchasing meeting then cycle distribution meeting, Hindi weeks meeting, safety committee meeting, VIP meeting, Technical meeting, sports meeting, Energy conservation meeting, award distribution committee meeting etc. A meeting takes minimum 3-4 hours and I have to attend all meeting being in charge. Apart from attending the meeting, I am also the member of several tender committee and inquiry committee thus didn't get time to read the proposal in details. And without reading properly I don't sign" replied Misharji almost in single breath

"But Mishraji, this job is also important and delay can't be afforded.." said big -boss

"Sir, delay was not because of me but of system." replied Misharji instantly

Big –boss knew Mishraji was a hardworking and sincere person thus without being angry said "Misharji, you are a senior officer thus somehow you have to manage all the things and find out some solutions".

"Sir, I suggest that in a week of 05 days, 03 days should be kept exclusively for meetings, presentation and similar sort of things while remaining 02 day for doing the work without any disturbance" suggested Mishraji.

URGENT FILE

"This case is urgent, it has to be done on top priority" ordered boss in one breathless voice

"Yes sir" replied the subordinate who was already reeling under so many "priorities"

"As it is urgent I want file of this case by tomorrow morning on my table" continued the boss

"But sir it is already 4' O clock and there is also one important case----

"No excuse, this is to be done on top priority", interrupted boss and hanged up the telephone

Mr. Bhola, the subdued subordinate, took deep sigh, cursed his boss and had a glance on his watch then rang up to his house to tell his wife that he would not come early in the evening as he had to sit late due to some urgent work thus scheduled visit to some relative's ceremony had to be cancel. Fed up with his frequent "urgent work" wife hang up without speaking a word.

Bhola remained thoughtful for a moment, thought about angry face of wife, complaints of children. He gave jerk to his head as though he wanted to throw home's out of his mind right now, then started the "top priority job".

In morning, he gave urgent file to boss.

"Good, that should be the spirit," said the boss, and beckoned Bhola to sit down "I usually tell people that we must work 200% of our capacity, you know our limit are stretchable" continued the boss.

Bhola knew very well that once boss comes in philosophical mood, simply you have to nod even if you don't agree with his philosophy. Thus he kept on enduring philosophy of boss on work ethics and sprit for half an hour.

Meantime another subordinate also entered in the boss's office and finding right opportunity Bhloa slipped out from the office.

Next day, Bhola got opportunity to get in the office of Boss. During discussion on some other issue Bhola noticed that that "Yesterday top priority file" for which he endured the anger of his wife and dismay of children, that very important and urgent file, was lying in the tray of Boss. Condition of file was giving clear indication that boss had not even touched it.

"Sir this file" said Bhola with polite dismay in his voice

"Yes, yes it is under deliberation before sending to HQ" said the boss with casual voice

"By the way, Bhola, what happened to that case which I gave yesterday"

"Sir, it will be over by tomorrow" said the Bhola

"No,Mr. Bhola I want it today itself, it is urgent" said boss with emphatic voice.

SHEPHERD

Meeting was going on but with a difference. Boss was not present in the meeting as he was on leave. But meeting has to be conducted because show must continue, as they say.

Now who will chair the meeting?

Temple without God statue cannot be called temple. Thus someone has to be anointed in the absence of main God for the temple of meetings.

And all eyes fixed on "next senior" not by suitability but by seniority in the pecking order.

Worth of measurement of any person in bureaucracy is seniority not his/ her suitability.

And who could be more senior than Mr. Jayaram. So what if he was not suitable for the post in people opinion. After all, seniority has to be respected, it was taught.

Mr. Jayaram was mild, sober and go slow type person. He never tried hard for anything. If he got something it was ok, if he did not get still it was ok. It was his bad luck that he always remained in second position, always stand by. Always took the orders to pass on to others down the line. An executor rather than maker of the things.

Nothing can be more damaging to your traits than being in the shadow of a banyan tree for long.

Thus today, by virtue of his being most senior, Mr. Jayaram became most suitable for anointing.

Everyone was happy

Mr. Jayaram was happy that he got the opportunity to sit on the coveted chair, albeit for few days

Others were happy because there would be "peace" at least for few days. After all, there was no need to fear from a Tiger without teeth.

And today he got the opportunity to take the decision and to give the order. He was nervous and not sure whether his decision was right or not, order was right or not. What would others think about him if decisions went wrong? He was perturbed and felt uncomfortable in coveted chair. He realized how easy it was to pass on the order of others down the line. Easy to be critical of others decision but difficult to take our own affecting many.

How easy it is to be 'God' but how difficult it is to please everyone.

And how difficult it is to become Shepherd of human being, the most treacherous creature in the world.

TAMING THE BULL

“Sir, last week I made a complaint against Mr. A for misbehaving and insubordination “asked Mr. Grudge with resentment in his voice

Boss did not speak anything but beckoned Mr. Grudge to sit down and ordered for two cup of tea and said “So what do you want Mr. Grudge?

“Sir,I want this person Mr. A to be penalized for misbehavior to set a precedent for others”

Boss, a seasoned person, known for his wisdom and managerial capabilities looked towards Mr. Grudge and said

“Mr. Grudge in any company, be it govt. or private, there are three type of employees. First one is *born- sincere* type. Give them any work they will do it with full sincerity without asking or troubling much to others. Second types are *carrot - stick sincere* i.e. they are made to be sincere by stick or carrot policy. They are not motivated but have to be kept motivated by one ways or others. Third one is born critics or trouble creator. It is third types who creates maximum problem in the company. Instead of work and let others work they believe in creating and enjoying problem to get importance. The real skill of a manger is not in managing first and second type of employees but to third type also to maintain an atmosphere of work and peace. While first and second type can be manage easily to get job done but third one cannot be unless they are given some sort of recognition or undue importance, which is always not possible."

"Sir, except Mr. A, everyone is helping and co-operating with me and doing the work sincerely. It in only Mr. A, who is making atmosphere polluted with his impudence. If you transfer him –

Boss waved him to stop and said "Ordering the transfer will not solve the problem. Only location of problem will change. Lot of din will be made without any meaningful output. I want you should learn certain thing about managing the different type of people as you have to go a long way. Ignoring the nonsense of the people is also one way of managing them particularly of third type. If you can't control them then simply ignore them."

"Sir, I am not getting you"

"Mr. Grudge, we all are working in govt. company where some people are like bull or simply govt. bull having enormous power and protection due to various internal and extraneous reasons.

Don't waste your time and energy in taming such bulls. Simply ignore and avoid these always ready to fight govt. bull"

"It means one should feared them and let them allow to do all short of nonsense "said Mr. Grudge in angered tone

"Avoiding or ignoring does not mean fearing but managing the things. You can't afford to lose 98% due to 2%. You are not a reformer. You are a manager and thus must know how to manage either by stick, carrot or by ignoring, depend upon where you stand and what is at stake" advised boss patiently

"It means it is not possible to take any actions against them and one should only continue to ignore their nonsense forever" asked Mr. Grudge disgustedly

"If you ever hit your back to wall only then take action whatever you feel fit, and that time don't listen to anybody including me also. Till then you must learn to stay away from them and not to wave red cloth by taking action against them. A good manager must learn not to be "hit" by these govt. bulls."

FICTITIOUS SINCERITY

They were always in top gear of their sincerity when there was no work or work of less significance. And when there was demand for real sincerity for some work of importance and responsibilities either these 'fictitious sincere' hide themselves in some safe corner -like the reptile sensing the danger. Or show up as busy in some other work.

The other basic quality of these fictitious sincere person is they tends to display their power to weak ones or their juniors and that too in the presence of other persons. Moreover as soon as they see their boss or some senior persons around they become hyperactive in their activities to show their sincerity. They start shouting unnecessary on juniors and start roaming here and there without any work or reasons. Their basic objective is to show the boss how sincere and concern they are in their work to impress the boss. They are very quick in arranging tea or snacks or throwing party to seniors. They hardly contribute anything real positive or of value by the end of the day for the company but show how tired they became. They believe in controlling the people under them and highly demanding for respect from their juniors.

These fictitious sincere persons have a real sincerity in monitoring others or repeating the words of their boss. In fact they work as repeater stations of boss. They have outstanding memory in remembering what someone said on what occasion but hardly remembered anything related with work. These parasites always ready for excuse in case of something goes wrong and remain in front line to take the credit.

And where on the earth such parasites will find shelter and scope to grow than in Govt. Company. After all, there is always enough space to adjust incompetency and tolerance for insincerity for such parasites in the Company as sycophants and 'Sevek' are always in demand there.

JOB COMPLETED BUT ----

The story is like two persons were working on road side in burning sun, one was digging the holes and second person standing just behind of him filled up the hole after some time of completion of the digging of hole. This activity of digging of holes and filling them continued with full attention and caring that and all holes should be at equidistance.

Seeing this activity without productivity, one onlooker asked to explain. First person replied I had been engaged for digging the holes and will get the payment based on total number of holes dug. Second person replied I was asked to fill up the dug holes and will get the payment accordingly.

"But what exactly you are planning to do by this digging and filling up holes activity in this strong Sun." inquired the onlooker

"Sir Job is given to us for *planting the sampling* but what we can do? Sampling- planter is on leave and we have the instruction to complete the job earliest possible to get the salary."

In Govt. Company also things are akin of 'digging of holes and filling them.' That is, one digs a hole during the day and then another fills it up at night ; the next day there is zero output but two salaries are paid. This is the 'activity without productivity

(Who knows tomorrow water - giver also come and will get the payment for watering the 'plants' for extended period.)

And later on inquiring, it would conclude that all plants were grazed by stray bovine and recommendation given to put barbed wire enclosure for plants and engaging the watchman round the clock.)

RECESSION –PROOF

In govt. offices, three things are hardly hit by any recession, global or local.

1. Xerox - Whether office be paper less or not but Xerox is something that hardly hit by any recession as there are always many circular, amendment to be kept in hard copy even though available in soft copy but hard copy has more weight (of authenticity) then soft one. Who knows tomorrow computer may be hit by some deadly virus having some enigmatic name. There are also many paper collectors who believe in keeping one copy of anything official and two copies of everything personal on official account. Having this liberty is bona fide official right Further if there is not enough Xerox bill in boss's name then it gives iota of doubt that boss is not having enough work in hand or may be sidelined by super-boss.

2. Chaiwala (Tea vendor) - Whether inaugural or farewell, meetings or seminars,flood or drought, tea is an integral part of any office. There is always scope of tea in every season and

occasion and no meetings can be concluded without tea. How big are you in the pecking order or in hierarchy depend on your bill of tea.

3. Photowala (Photographer) – A picture speaks thousand words. Thus whether you do anything or not do but you must be in photo that too in front line. Be it inauguration, distribution, farewell, visiting of good for nothing dignitaries, energy conservation, safety week, vigilance week, Hindi fortnight, ladies club, officers club, union meeting, officers meeting etc. Thus there is always a scope of photographer in govt. offices from 1 January to 31 Dec without fear of recession.

As no offices is complete without these recession proof utilities, thus time is not far away when above three utilities will be declared as essential services under ESMA (Essential Service Maintenance Act) by Govt. notification.

EXPERIENCED MANAGER

His versatility was undisputed.
His experience was unchallenged.
His analytical ability was unparalleled.

But all this meant for finding the mistakes of others rather than in doing the work of any worth, in creating the roadblock rather than clearing them. For him, winning was important not the right or wrong.

A lawyer in the skin of manager, enjoying an important position, by virtue of his experience in years rather than his contribution to the Company.

He had the experience of working in more than a dozen private companies –and finally settled in one Govt. company.

"More companies you see, more experienced you become" he used to say and repeatedly boast about his experience of earlier companies he had worked with and resigned (or thrown out).

One who listen his 'experience- stories' patiently got his signature on any damn file. And, if someone dares to argue or not listened him seriously bound to face his wrath. Others have no choice but bear him, listened him and adjust with him. After all he was holding important position.

And the experienced manager was doing well, enjoying well and progressing well. After all, as Patriotism is the last refuge of scoundrels so the Govt. Company is also last refuge of such 'Experienced Manager'.

SECOND THOUGHT

Give a second thought to following management jargon

"We will do it"

Means

You will do it.

"You have done a great job"

Means

More work to be given to you.

"We are a team"

Means

I am not to be blamed if thing goes wrong.

"That is actually a good question"

Means

I do not know anything of worth about it

"All the best"

Means

You are in the trouble in coming time

"You are the best person around who can do it"

Means

You are the only donkey around who can carry this weight.